STEPHEN NIELSON
-and-
OVID YOUNG
-present-

GLORIOUS IS THY NAME

FOR TWO PIANOS

Parts for two pianos or piano-organ duet are included in this collection. If two pianos are used, Piano I plays from the pull-out section and Piano II plays from the main volume. If piano and organ are used, Organ plays from the pull-out section and Piano plays Piano I part from the main volume.

Possession of a CCLI license does not grant you permission to make copies of this music. For clarification about the rights CCLI does grant you, please call 1-800-234-2446.

© Copyright 1999 Van Ness Press, Inc. (ASCAP).
Distributed by Church Street Music, (a div. of GMG)
Nashville, Tennessee, 37234.

STEPHEN NIELSON and OVID YOUNG, having recently celebrated their silver anniversary as a musical team, continue to be one of the most active duo-piano ensembles of our time. Since their first concert together as faculty artists at Olivet University in Illinois, they have played some 3,000 performances throughout the United States, Canada, England, Germany, France, Austria, Russia, Switzerland, the Czech Republic and the Caribbean.

The venues of Nielson & Young's many years of performances have been incredibly varied, including major concert halls, college and university campuses, cathedrals, churches and synagogues, convention centers, ocean-going cruise ships and television studios. They have several duo-piano recordings to their credit. Individually, they have recorded as solo artists, in some cases with orchestra.

Subsequent to their concurrent teaching appointments in Illinois, Stephen served for several years on the music faculties of the University of Texas at Dallas and the Southern Methodist University Summer Conservatory. Ovid has taught at Westmont College in California and Anderson University near Indianapolis, and presently serves as Adjunct Lecturer in Music at Olivet University near Chicago.

Stephen and his wife, Carolyne, reside in Dallas with their young daughters, Christiana and Caroline. Ovid and Laura Young live in Carrolton, Texas near their two sons, Kirk and Erik.

CONTENTS

All Glory, Laud, and Honor 30

Come, Thou Fount of Every Blessing 65

Glorious Is Thy Name Medley 4

Look, Ye Saints! The Sight Is Glorious 26

Praise God, from Whom All Blessings Flow 39

Redeemed 58

Take Thou My Hand and Lead Me 51

The Lord's My Shepherd 45

When I Survey the Wondrous Cross 18

Glorious Is Thy Name Medley
Glorious Name

B. B. McKINNEY
Duo-Piano Setting by
Stephen Nielson and Ovid Young

© Copyright 1942. Renewal 1970 Broadman Press (SESAC).
This Arr. © Copyright 1999 Broadman Press in *Glorious Is Thy Name*.
Distributed by Church Street Music (a div. of GMG), Nashville, TN 37234.

*"Breathe on Me," Tune, TRUETT, © Copyright 1937. Renewal 1965 Broadman Press (SESAC). All rights reserved.

*"Wherever He Leads I'll Go," Tune, FALLS CREEK, © Copyright 1936. Renewal 1964 Broadman Press (SESAC). All rights reserved.

Glorious Is Thy Name Medley — 14

18

*Commissioned by the Royal Lane Baptist Church, Dallas, Texas,
in honor of their pianist, Garey Wisdom, for ten years of faithful service to their music ministry.*

When I Survey the Wondrous Cross
Hamburg

LOWELL MASON
Duo-Piano Setting by
Stephen Nielson and Ovid Young

© Copyright 1999 Van Ness Press, Inc. (ASCAP) in *Glorious Is Thy Name*.
Distributed by Church Street Music (a div. of GMG), Nashville, TN 37234.

When I Survey the Wondrous Cross — 2

When I Survey the Wondrous Cross — 4

When I Survey the Wondrous Cross — 5

When I Survey the Wondrous Cross — 6

When I Survey the Wondrous Cross — 8

Look, Ye Saints! The Sight Is Glorious
Bryn Calfaria

WILLIAM OWEN
Duo-Piano Setting by
Stephen Nielson and Ovid Young

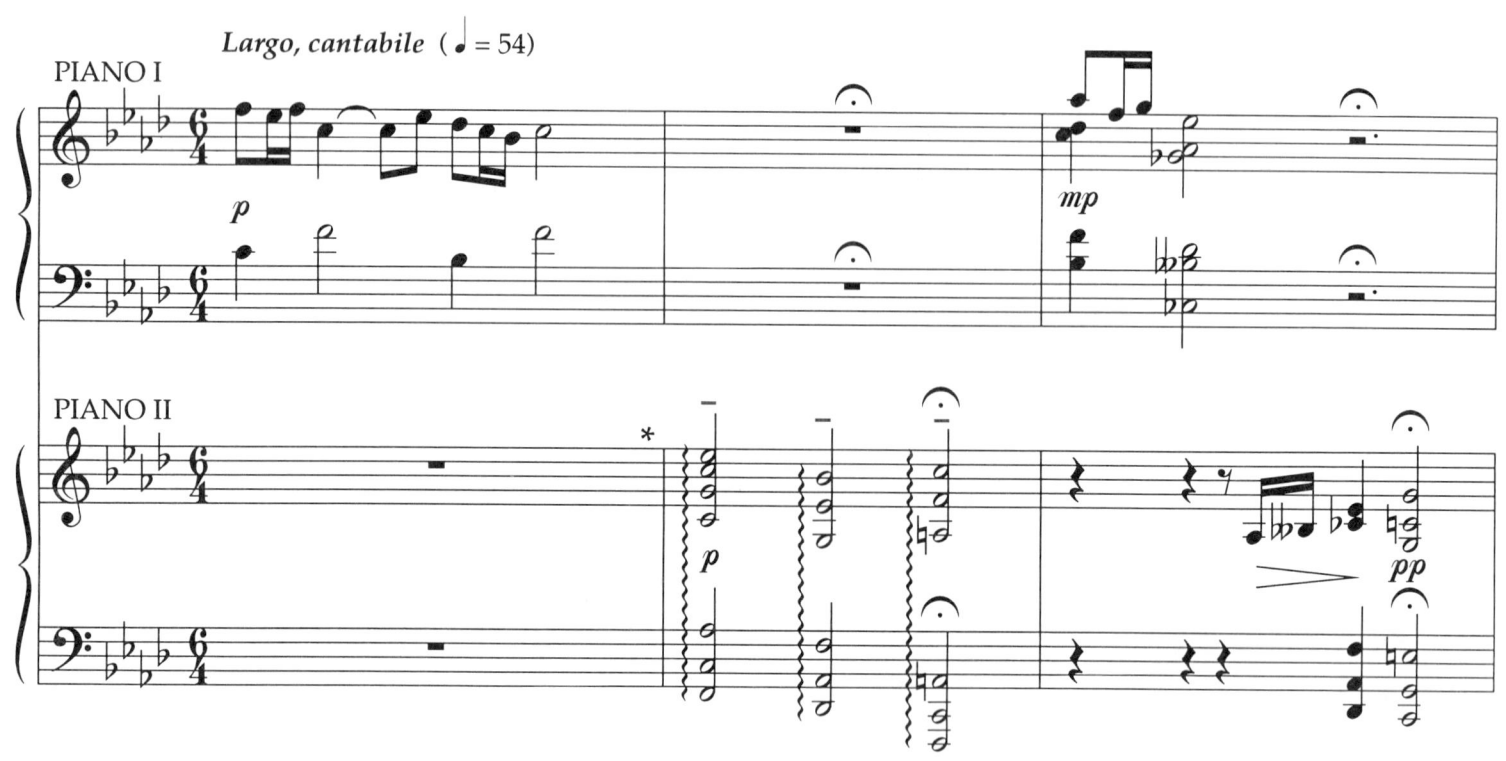

*Slowly rolled chords

© Copyright 1999 Van Ness Press, Inc. (ASCAP) in *Glorious Is Thy Name*.
Distributed by Church Street Music (a div. of GMG), Nashville, TN 37234.

Look, Ye Saints! The Sight Is Glorious — 2

Look, Ye Saints! The Sight Is Glorious — 4

All Glory, Laud, and Honor
St. Theodulph

MELCHIOR TESCHNER
Duo-Piano Setting by
Stephen Nielson and Ovid Young

© Copyright 1999 Van Ness Press, Inc. (ASCAP) in *Glorious Is Thy Name*.
Distributed by Church Street Music (a div. of GMG), Nashville, TN 37234.

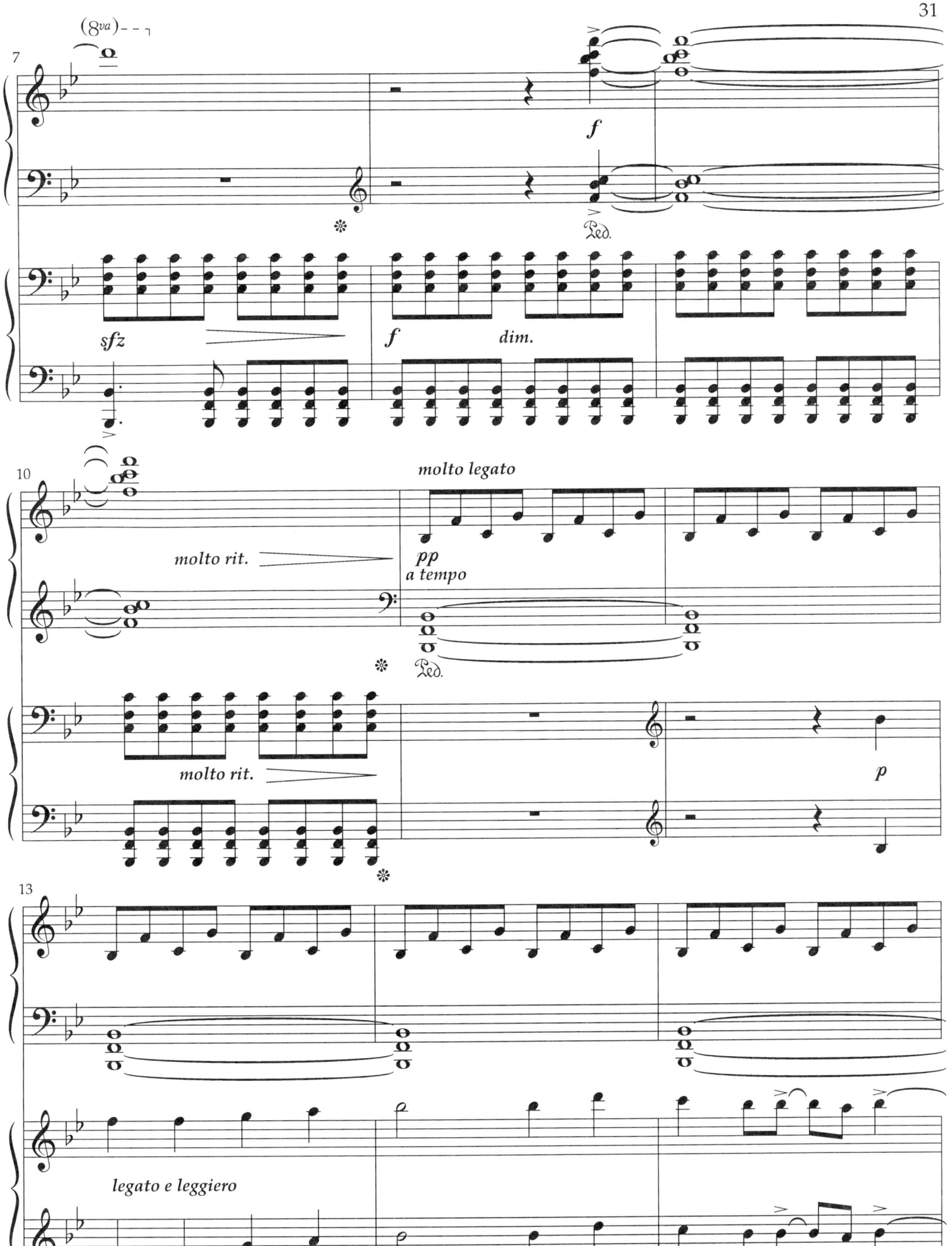

All Glory, Laud, and Honor — 2

All Glory, Laud, and Honor — 5

All Glory, Laud, and Honor — 6

All Glory, Laud, and Honor — 7

STEPHEN NIELSON
- and -
OVID YOUNG
- present -

GLORIOUS IS THY NAME
FOR PIANO AND ORGAN

CONTENTS

All Glory, Laud, and Honor 38

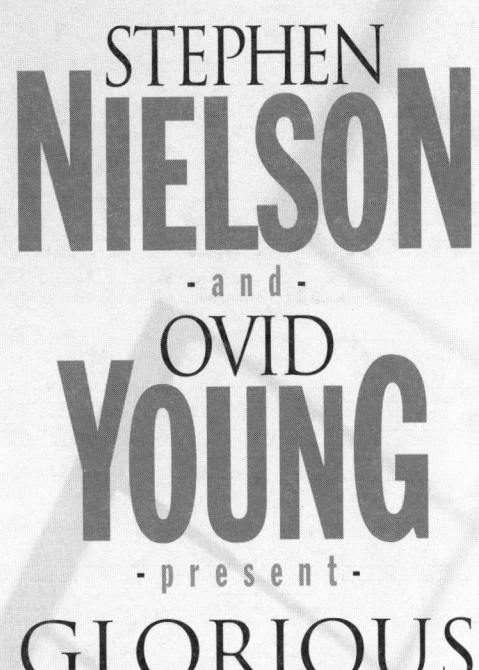

Come, Thou Fount of Every Blessing 86

Glorious Is Thy Name Medley 2

Look, Ye Saints! The Sight Is Glorious 33

Praise God, from Whom All Blessings Flow 51

Redeemed 76

Take Thou My Hand and Lead Me 67

The Lord's My Shepherd 59

When I Survey the Wondrous Cross 22

Parts for two pianos or piano-organ duet are included in this collection. If two pianos are used, Piano I plays from the pull-out section and Piano II plays from the main volume. If piano and organ are used, Organ plays from the pull-out section and Piano plays Piano I part from the main volume.

© Copyright 1999 Van Ness Press, Inc. (ASCAP).
Distributed by Church Street Music (a div. of GMG),
Nashville, Tennessee, 37234.

Glorious Is Thy Name Medley
Glorious Name

Sw. Flutes 8', 4' and 2'
Gt. Principals 8', 4' and 2'
Ped. 16' and 8'

B. B. McKINNEY
Piano-Organ Duet Setting by
Stephen Nielson and Ovid Young

© Copyright 1942. Renewal 1970 Broadman Press (SESAC).
This Arr. © Copyright 1999 Broadman Press in *Glorious Is Thy Name*.
Distributed by Church Street Music (a div. of GMG), Nashville, TN 37234.

Glorious Is Thy Name Medley — 2

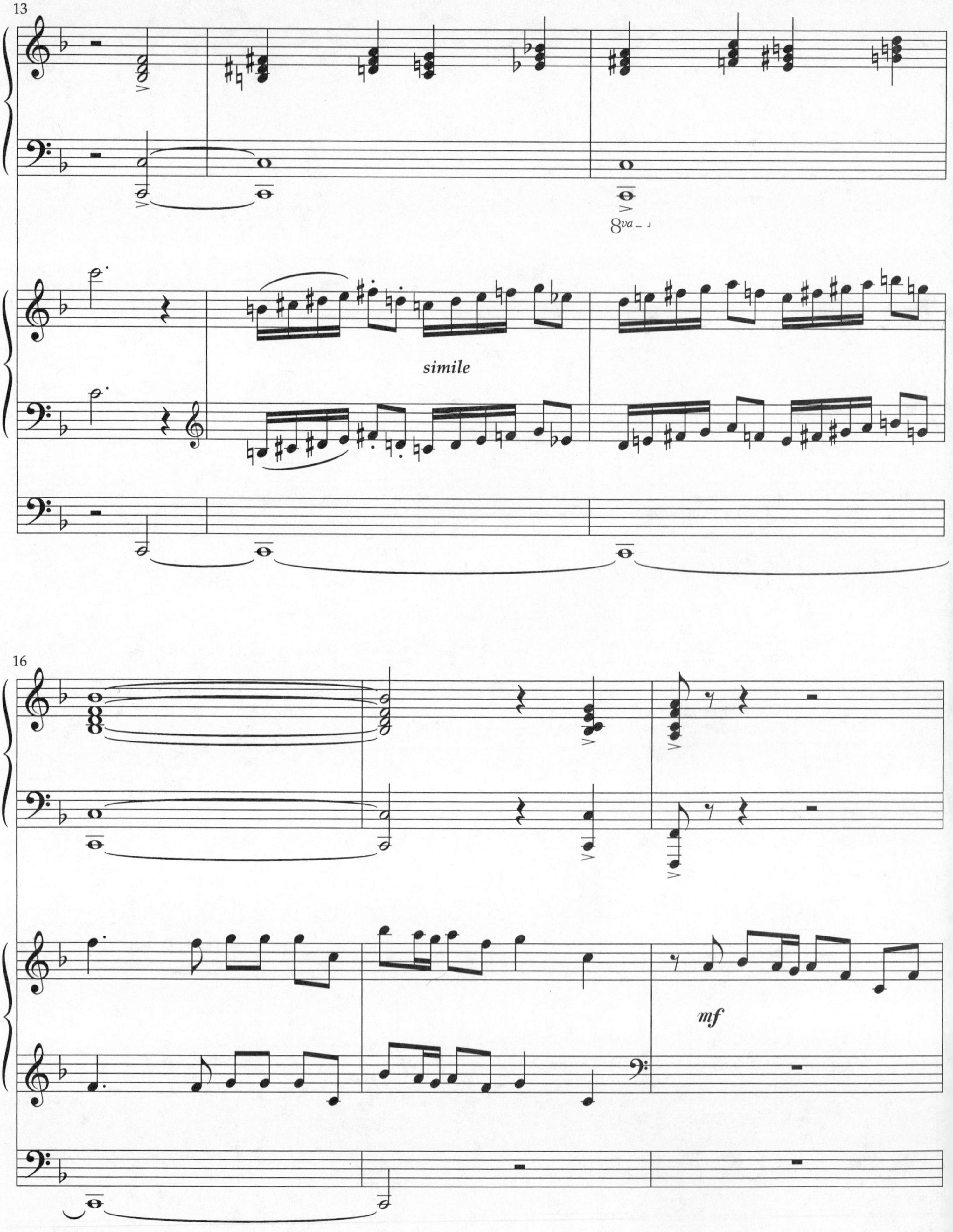
13
8va
simile
16
mf

Glorious Is Thy Name Medley — 4

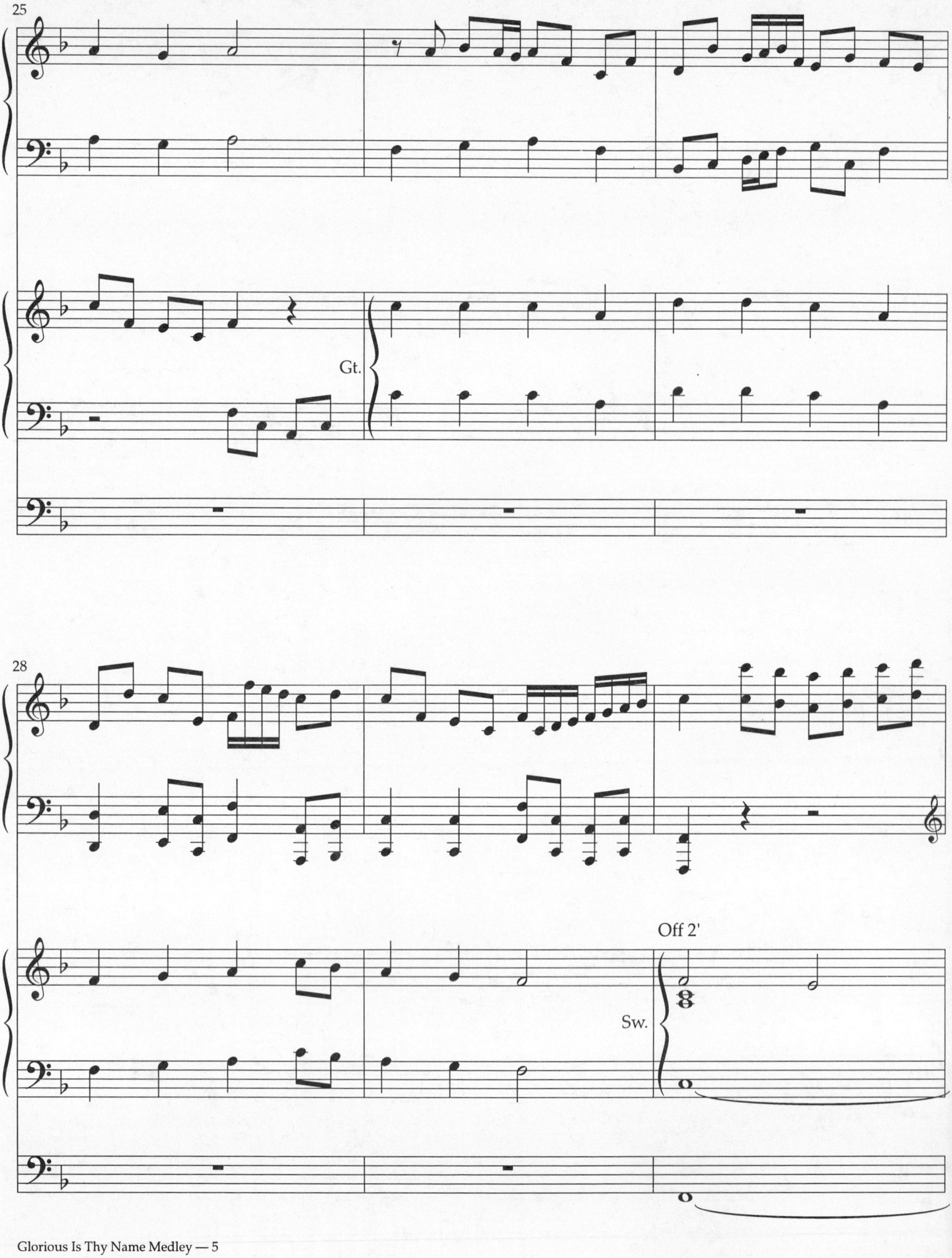
25
Gt.
28
Off 2'
Sw.

Glorious Is Thy Name Medley — 6

Glorious Is Thy Name Medley — 7

*"Breathe on Me," Tune, TRUETT, © Copyright 1937. Renewal 1965 Broadman Press (SESAC). All rights reserved.

Glorious Is Thy Name Medley — 8

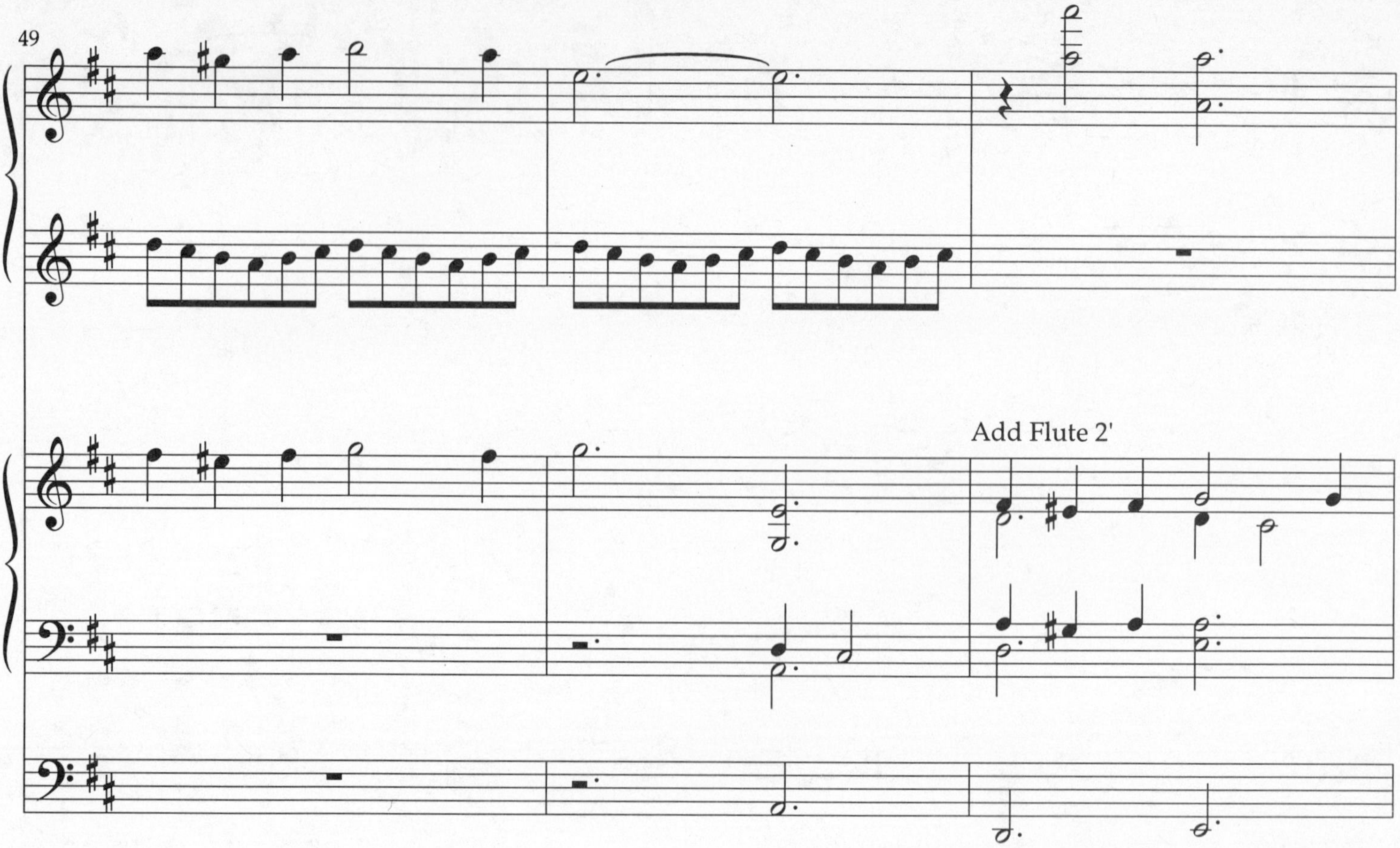
49
Add Flute 2'

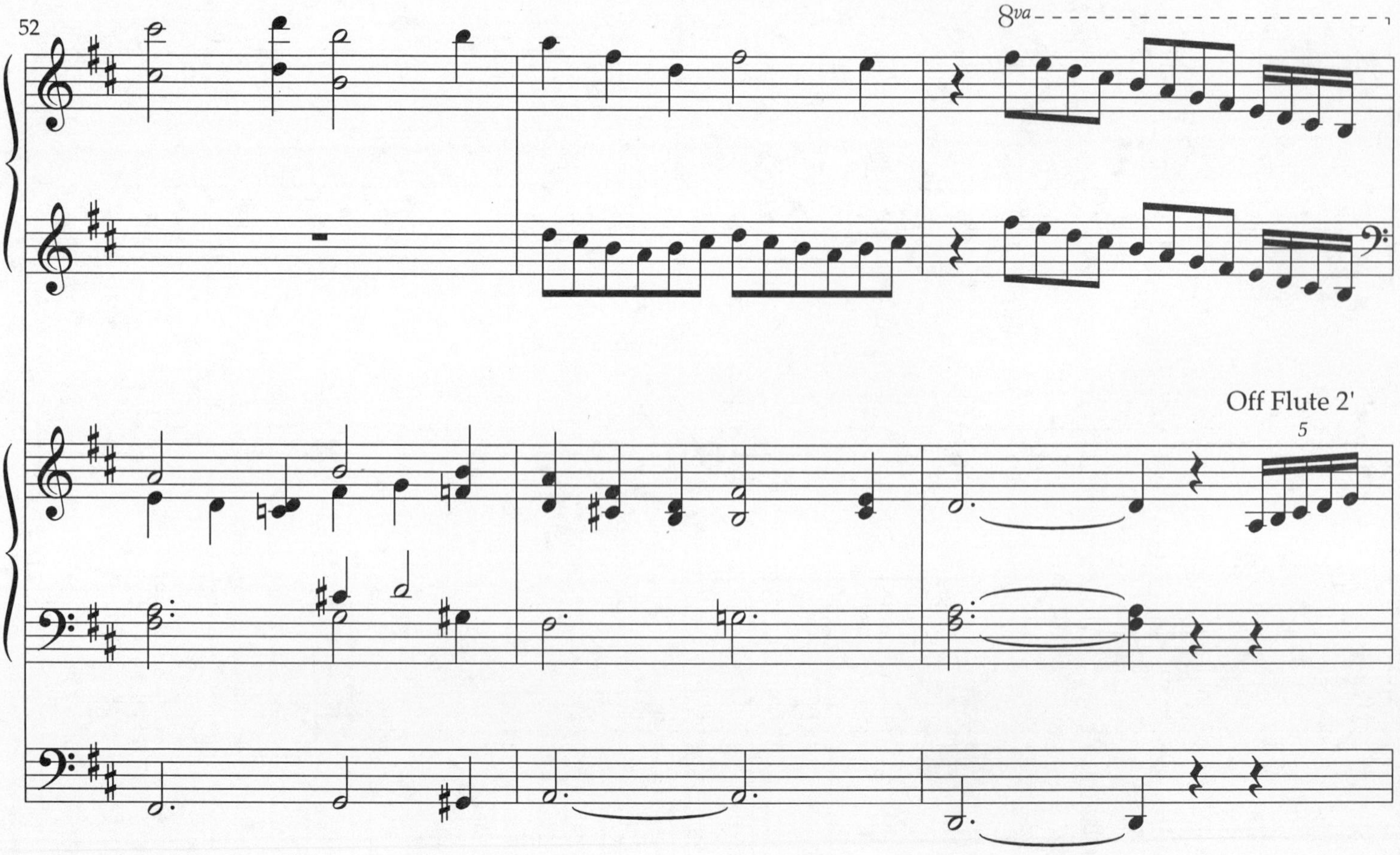
52
8va
Off Flute 2'
5

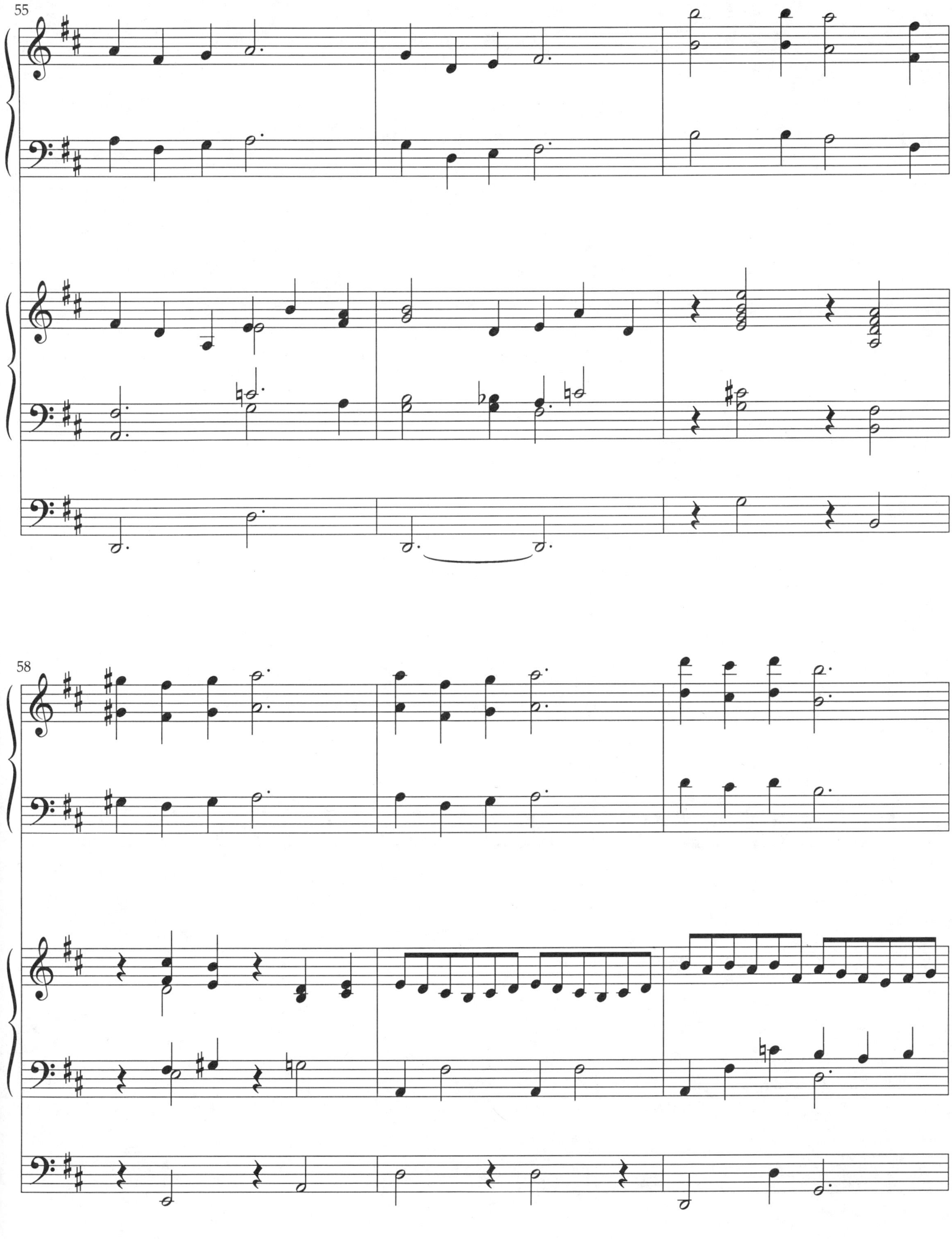
55
58

Glorious Is Thy Name Medley — 11

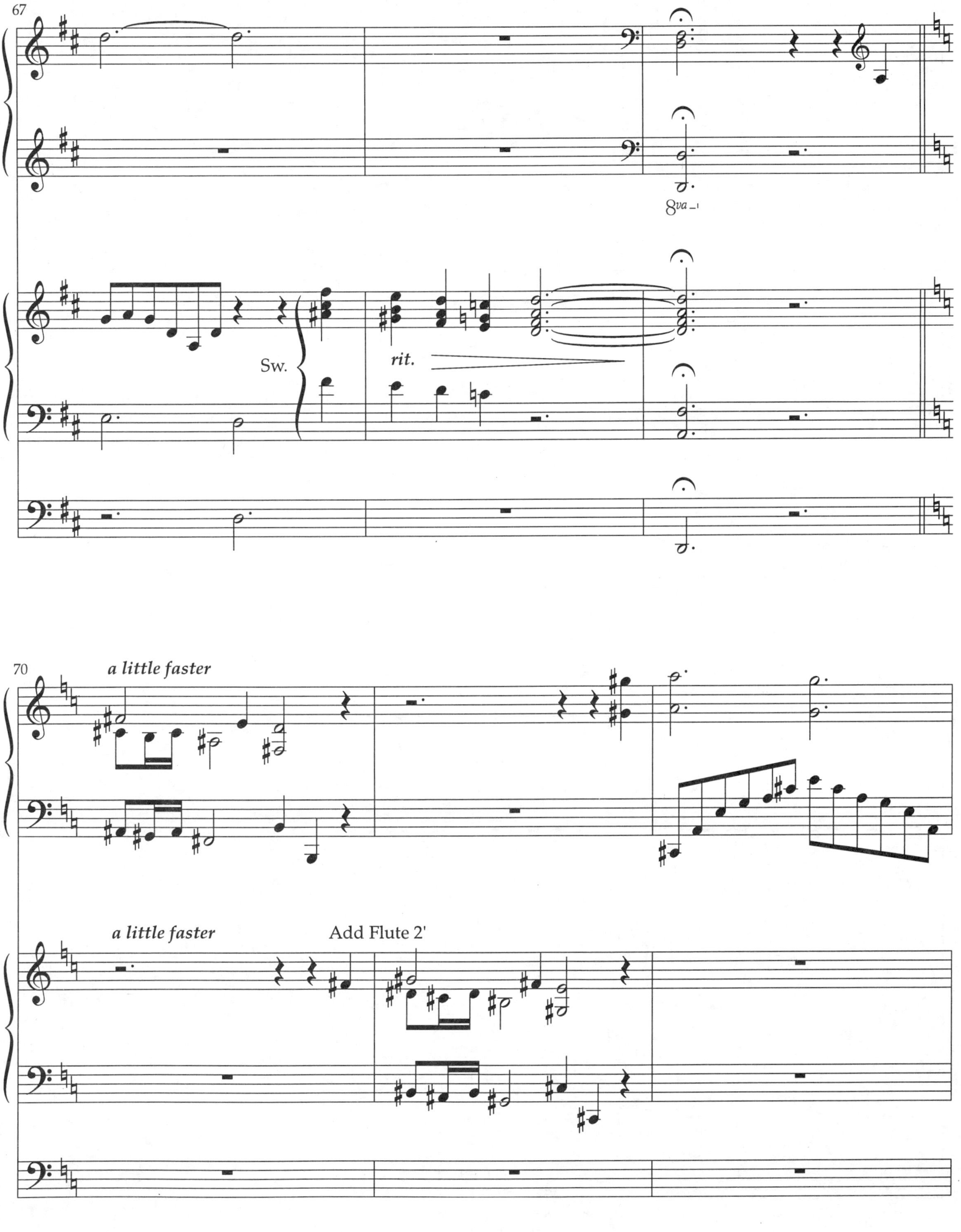
67
8va
Sw.
rit.
70
a little faster
a little faster
Add Flute 2'

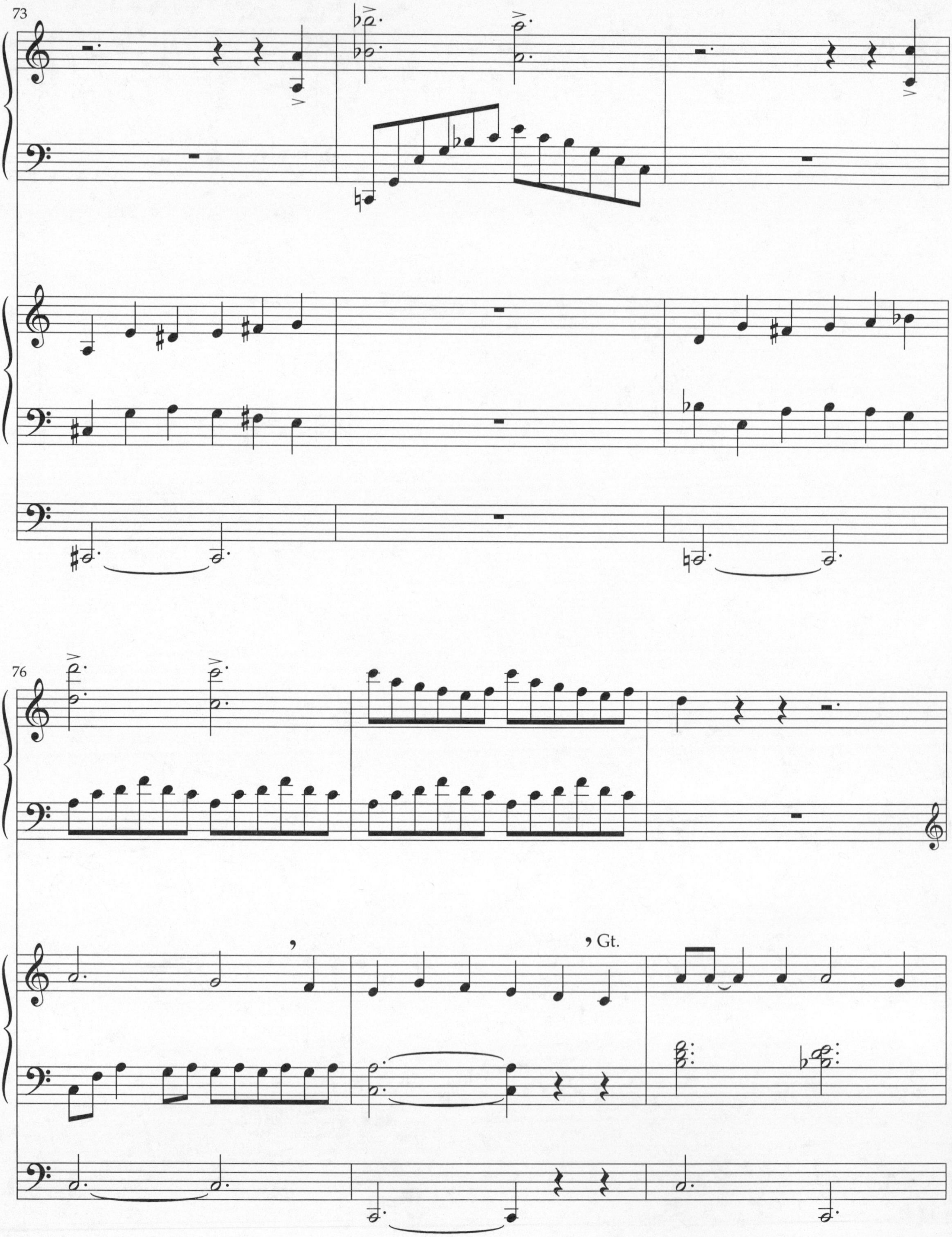
73
76
Gt.

*"Wherever He Leads I'll Go," Tune; FALLS CREEK. © Copyright 1936. Renewal 1964 Broadman Press (SESAC). All rights reserved.

Glorious Is Thy Name Medley — 14

Glorious Is Thy Name Medley — 15

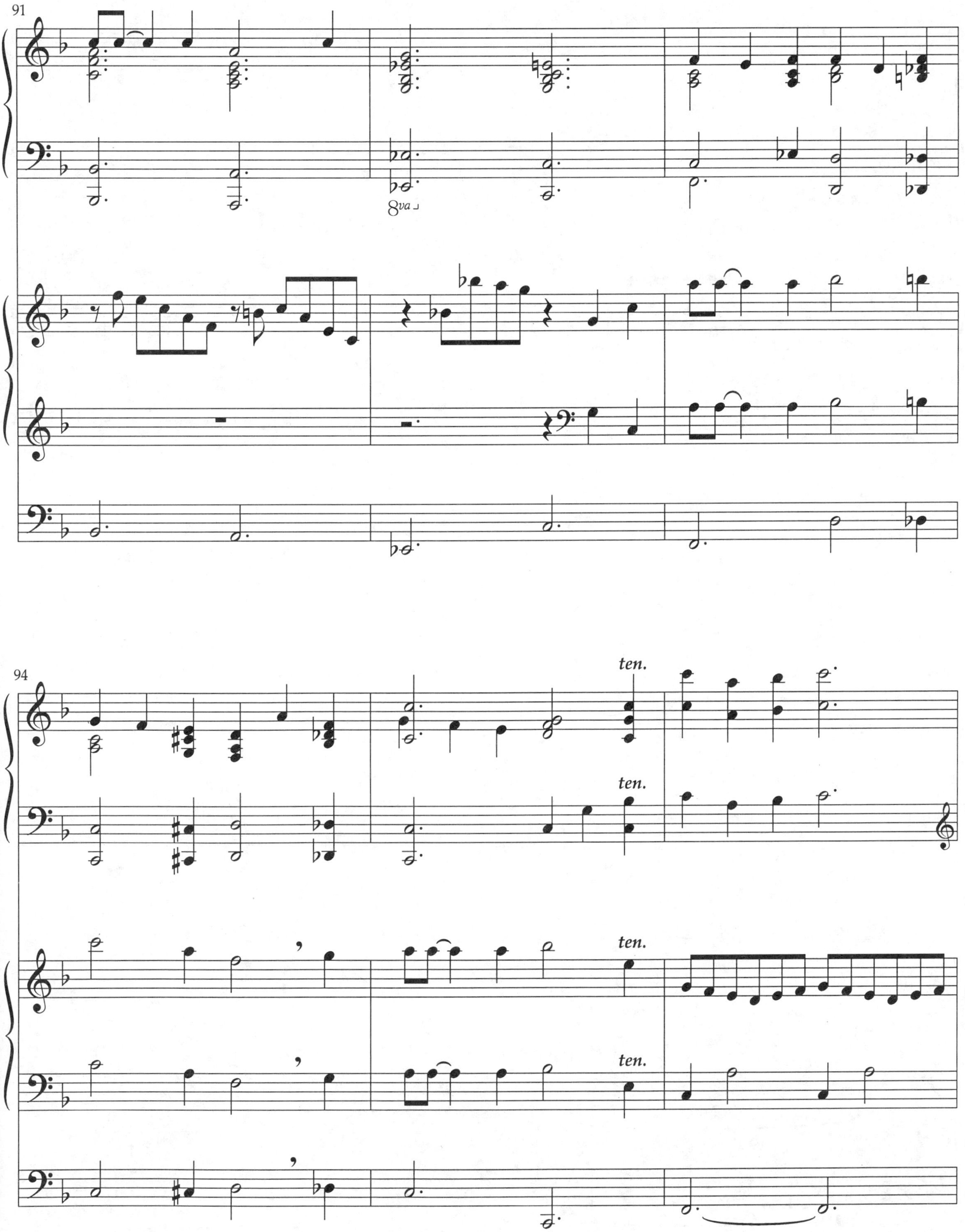
91
8va
94
ten.
ten.
ten.

Tempo I

Gt. Principals 8' and 4'

Glorious Is Thy Name Medley — 17

Glorious Is Thy Name Medley — 18

Glorious Is Thy Name Medley — 19

Glorious Is Thy Name Medley — 20

*Commissioned by the Royal Lane Baptist Church, Dallas, Texas,
in honor of their pianist, Garey Wisdom, for ten years of faithful service to their music ministry.*

When I Survey the Wondrous Cross
Hamburg

Sw.   Strings 8' and 4'
Gt.   Principal 8'
Ped.   16' and 8'

LOWELL MASON
Piano-Organ Duet Setting by
Stephen Nielson and Ovid Young

© Copyright 1999 Van Ness Press, Inc. (ASCAP) in *Glorious Is Thy Name*.
Distributed by Church Street Music (a div. of GMG), Nashville, TN 37234.

When I Survey the Wondrous Cross — 2

When I Survey the Wondrous Cross — 3

When I Survey the Wondrous Cross — 4

When I Survey the Wondrous Cross — 5

When I Survey the Wondrous Cross — 6

When I Survey the Wondrous Cross — 7

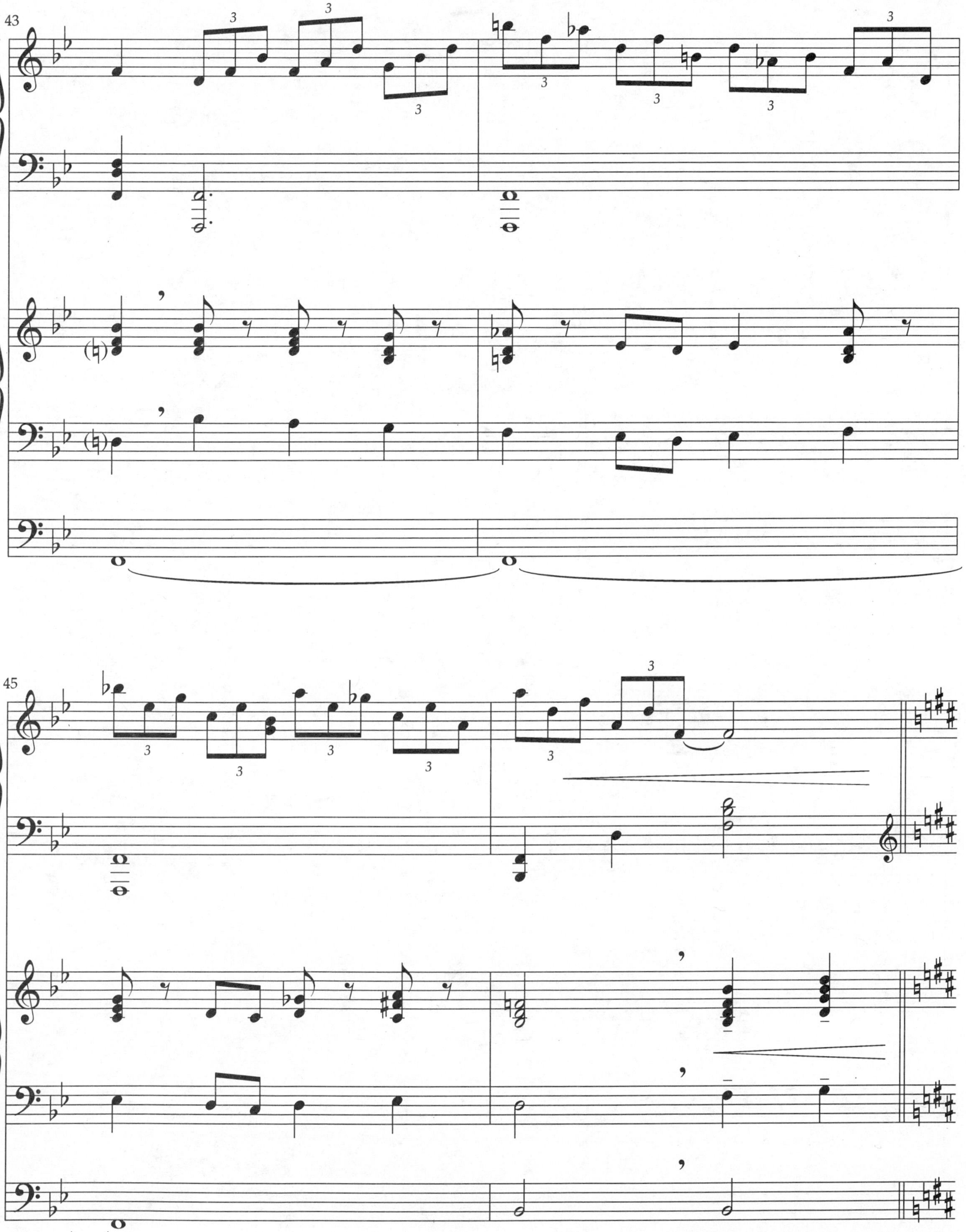
43
3
45
3

When I Survey the Wondrous Cross — 9

When I Survey the Wondrous Cross — 10

rit. to end

ten. ten.

arpeggiate slowly

p   *pp*

When I Survey the Wondrous Cross — 11

Look, Ye Saints! The Sight Is Glorious
Bryn Calfaria

Sw. Flutes and Strings 8' and 4'
Gt. Principals 8' and 4'
Ped. 16' and 8'

WILLIAM OWEN
Piano-Organ Duet Setting by
Stephen Nielson and Ovid Young

© Copyright 1999 Van Ness Press, Inc. (ASCAP) in *Glorious Is Thy Name*.
Distributed by Church Street Music (a div. of GMG), Nashville, TN 37234.

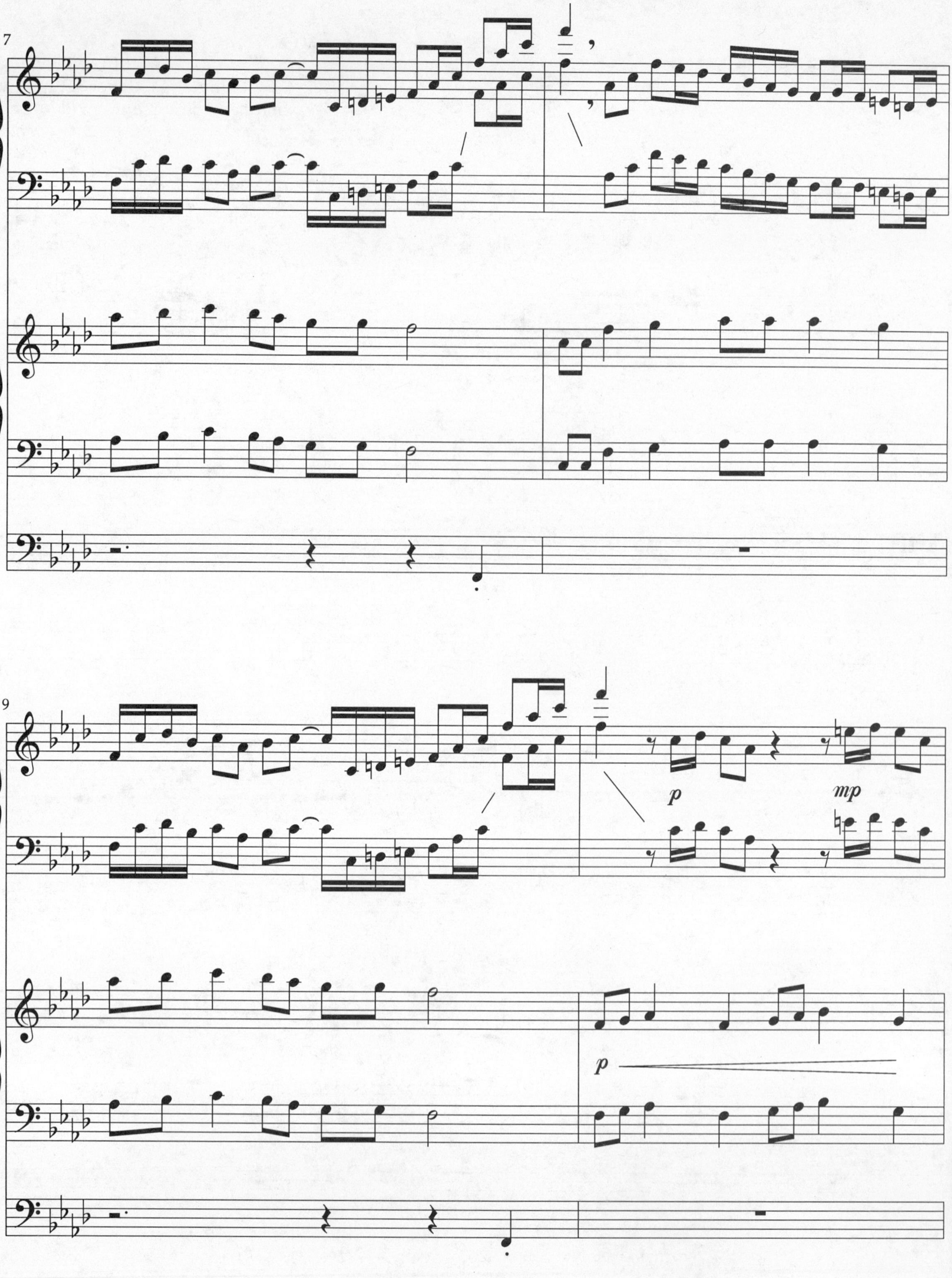
7
9
p
mp
p

Look, Ye Saints! The Sight Is Glorious — 3

Look, Ye Saints! The Sight Is Glorious — 4

Look, Ye Saints! The Sight Is Glorious — 5

All Glory, Laud, and Honor
St. Theodulph

Sw. Flutes 8' and 4'
Gt. Principals 8' and 4'
Ped. 16' and 8'

MELCHIOR TESCHNER
Piano-Organ Duet Setting by
Stephen Nielson and Ovid Young

© Copyright 1999 Van Ness Press, Inc. (ASCAP) in *Glorious Is Thy Name*.
Distributed by Church Street Music (a div. of GMG), Nashville, TN 37234.

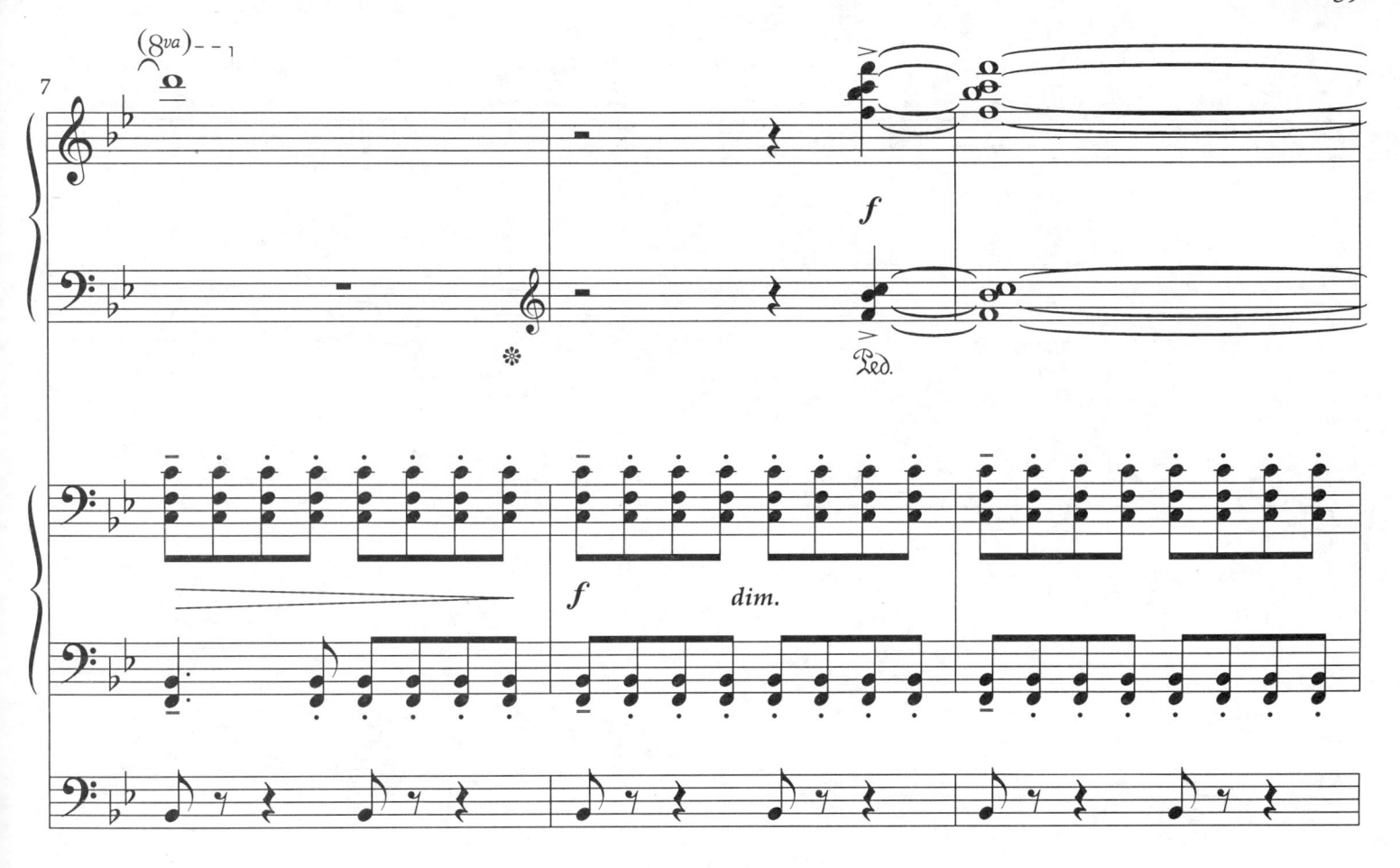

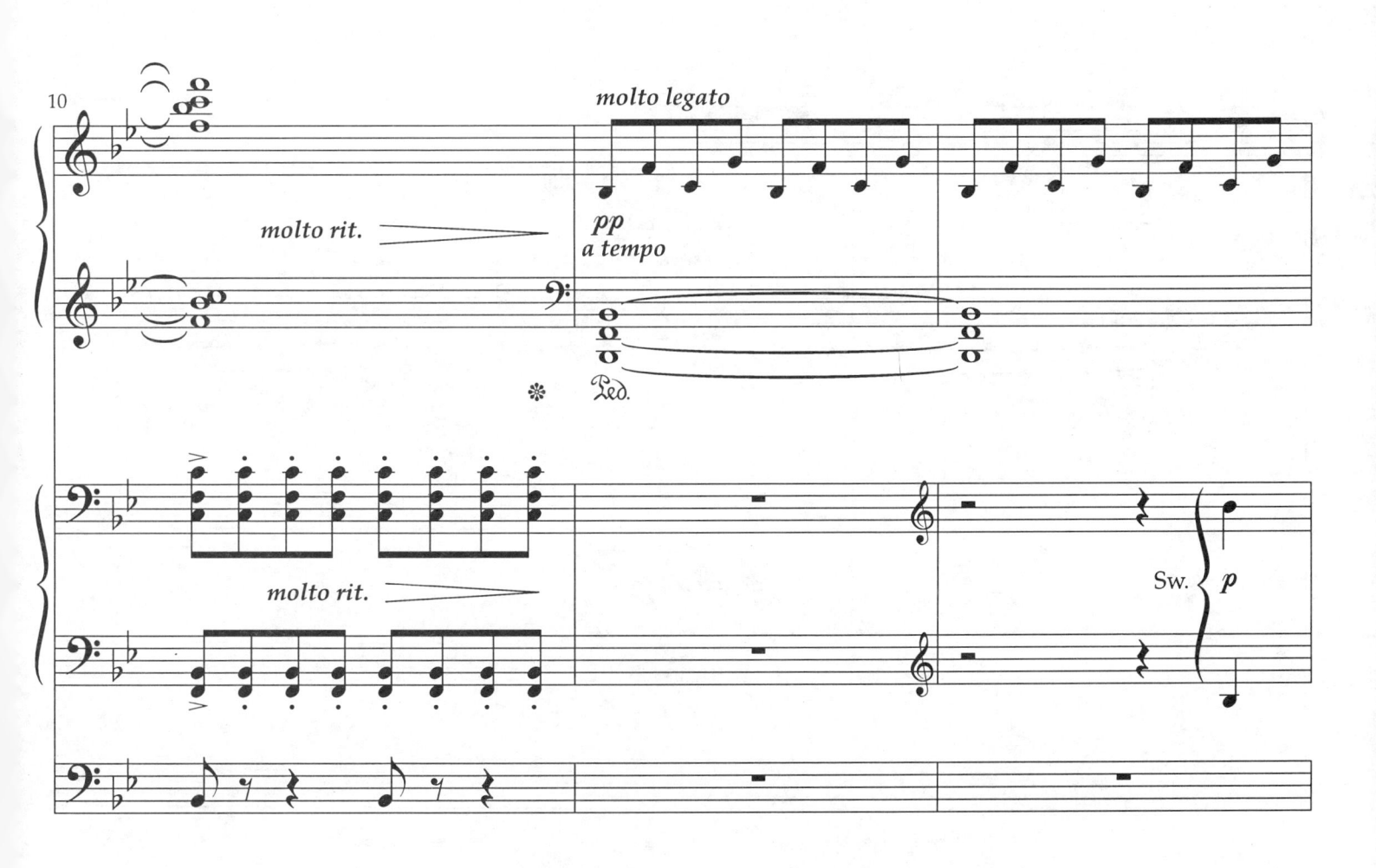

All Glory, Laud, and Honor — 2

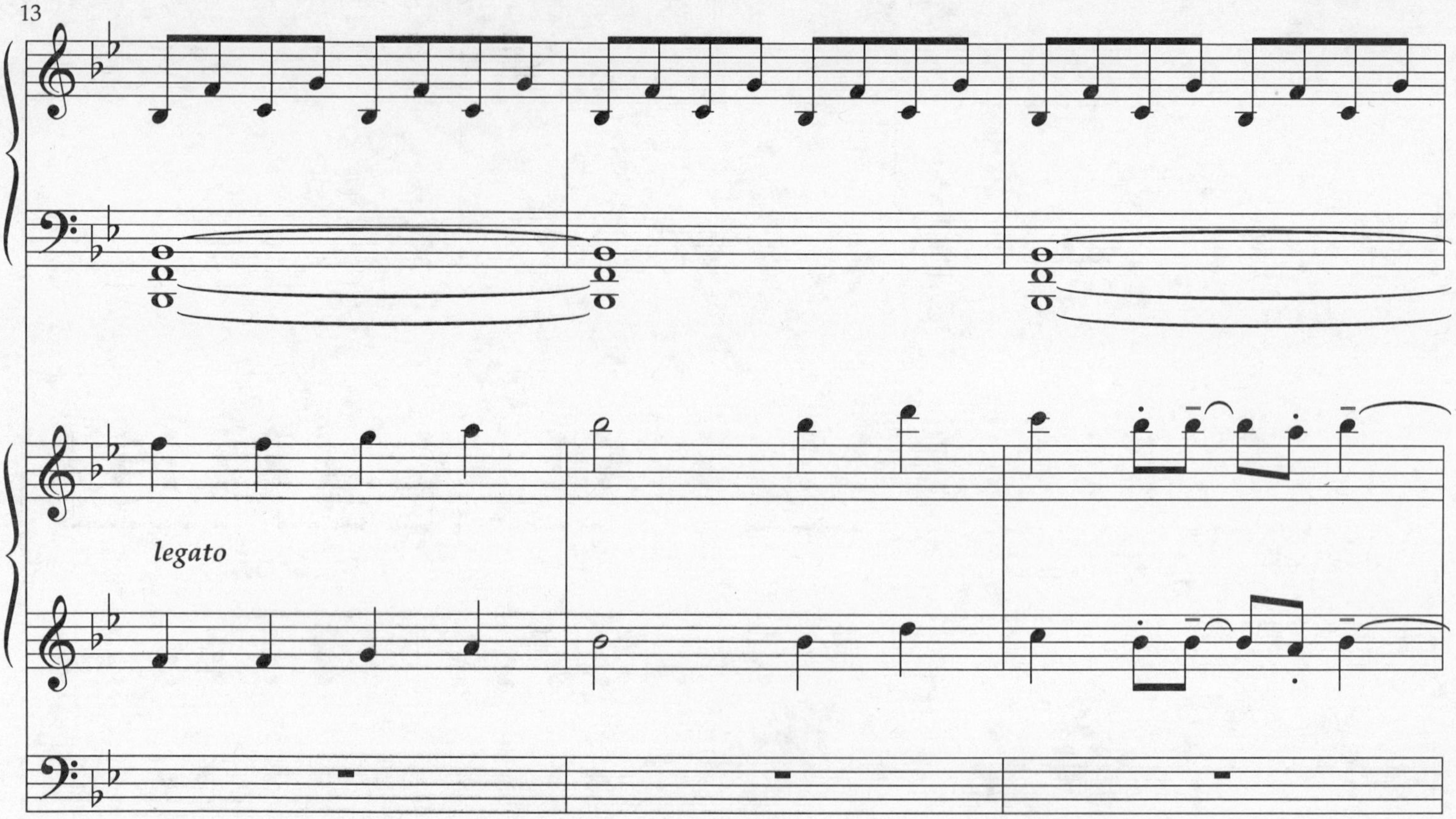
13
legato

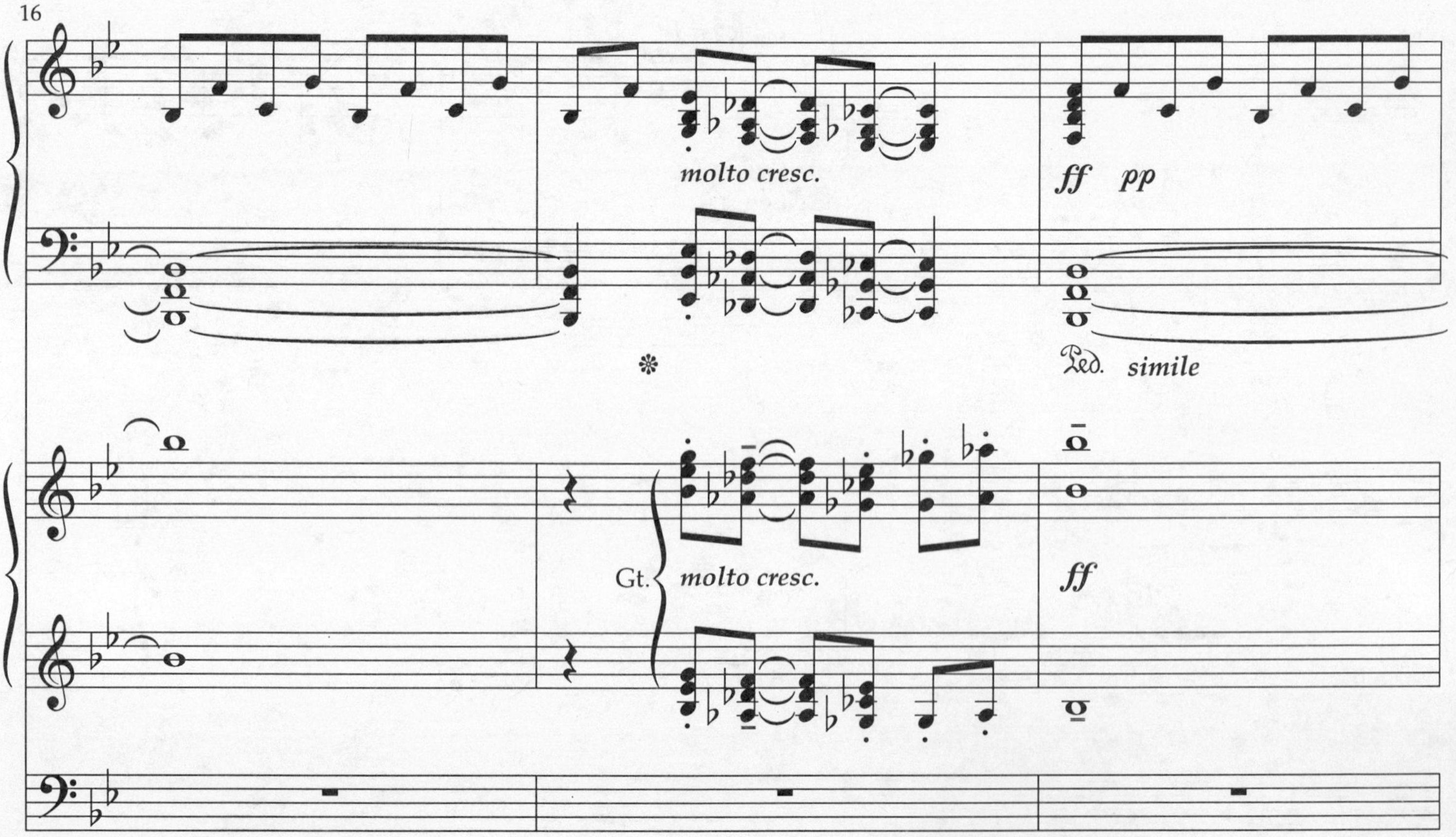
16
molto cresc.
ff
pp
Ped.
simile
Gt.
molto cresc.
ff

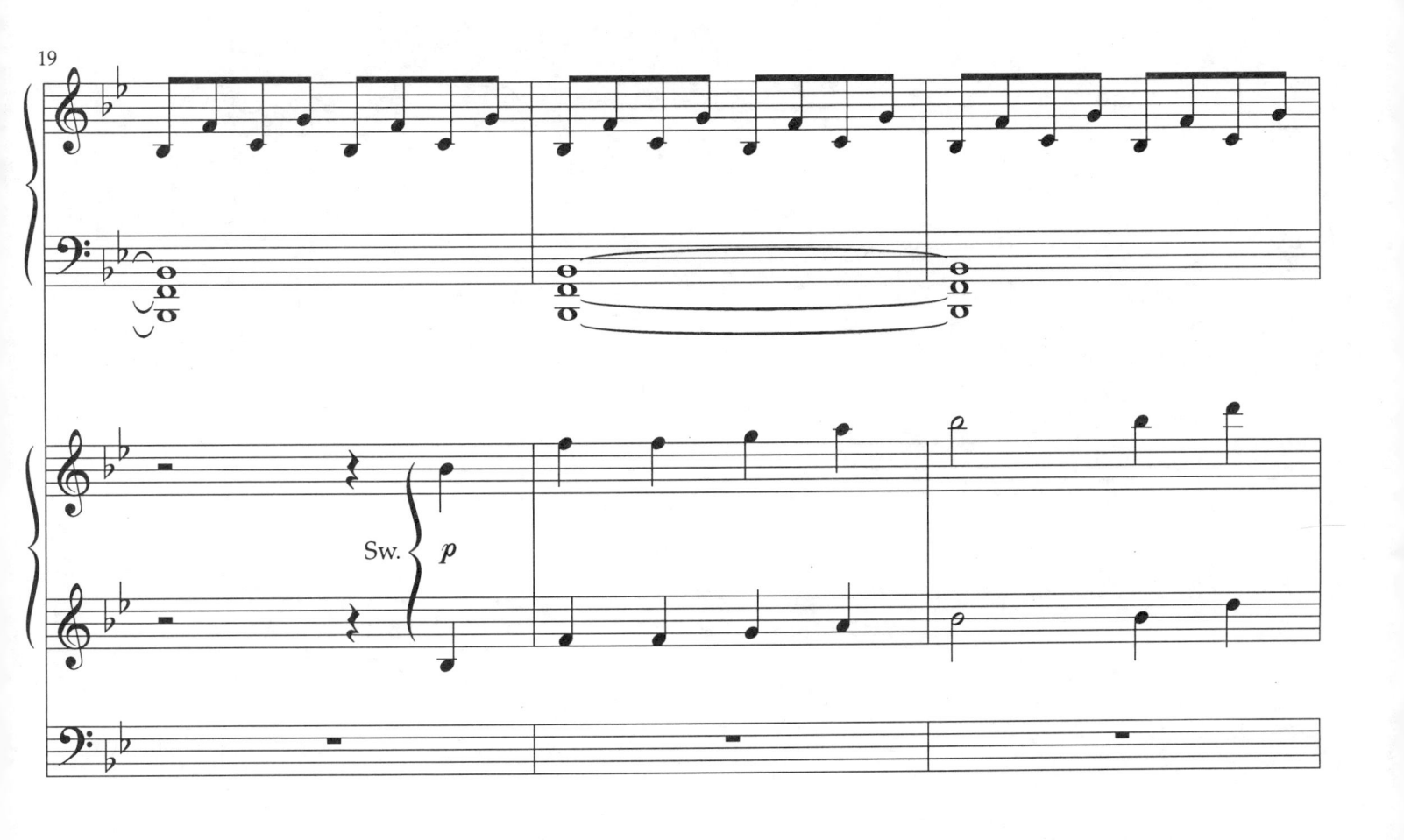

All Glory, Laud, and Honor — 4

All Glory, Laud, and Honor — 5

All Glory, Laud, and Honor — 6

molto legato; espressivo

All Glory, Laud, and Honor — 8

51
8va
a tempo
rit.
pp
a tempo
rit.
pp
55
attacca, energetically
f
ff
Add 2'
Gt.

All Glory, Laud, and Honor — 10

All Glory, Laud, and Honor — 11

68
meno mosso
mp
meno mosso
70
p
subito
ff
molto marcato
(p)
Gt.
subito
ff
molto marcato

72
8va
ff
molto rit.
ff
molto rit.

75
8va
a tempo
sfz
6
no rit.
fff
sfz
8va
8va
Full
a tempo
no rit.
fff

Praise God, from Whom All Blessings Flow
Old 100th

Sw. Reeds 8' and 4'
Gt. Principals 8' and 4'
Ped. 16' and 8'

Genevan Psalter, 1551 Edition
Piano-Organ Duet Setting by
Stephen Nielson and Ovid Young

© Copyright 1999 Van Ness Press, Inc. (ASCAP) in *Glorious Is Thy Name*.
Distributed by Church Street Music (a div. of GMG), Nashville, TN 37234.

Praise God, from Whom All Blessings Flow — 2

Praise God, from Whom All Blessings Flow — 3

Praise God, from Whom All Blessings Flow — 4

Praise God, from Whom All Blessings Flow — 5

Praise God, from Whom All Blessings Flow — 6

Praise God, from Whom All Blessings Flow — 7

8va
45
(♩ = 120-138)
ff
molto rit.
f Più mosso to end, with no rit.
Full
ff
molto rit.
f Più mosso to end, with no rit.
48
fff
5
sfz
fff

The Lord's My Shepherd
Brother James' Air

Sw. String and Flute 8' and 4'
Gt. Flutes 8' and 4'
Ped. 16' and 8'

J. L. MacBETH BAIN
Piano-Organ Duet Setting by
Stephen Nielson and Ovid Young

*Based on Arabesque #1 by Claude Debussy.

© Copyright 1999 Van Ness Press, Inc. (ASCAP) in *Glorious Is Thy Name*.
Distributed by Church Street Music (a div. of GMG), Nashville, TN 37234.

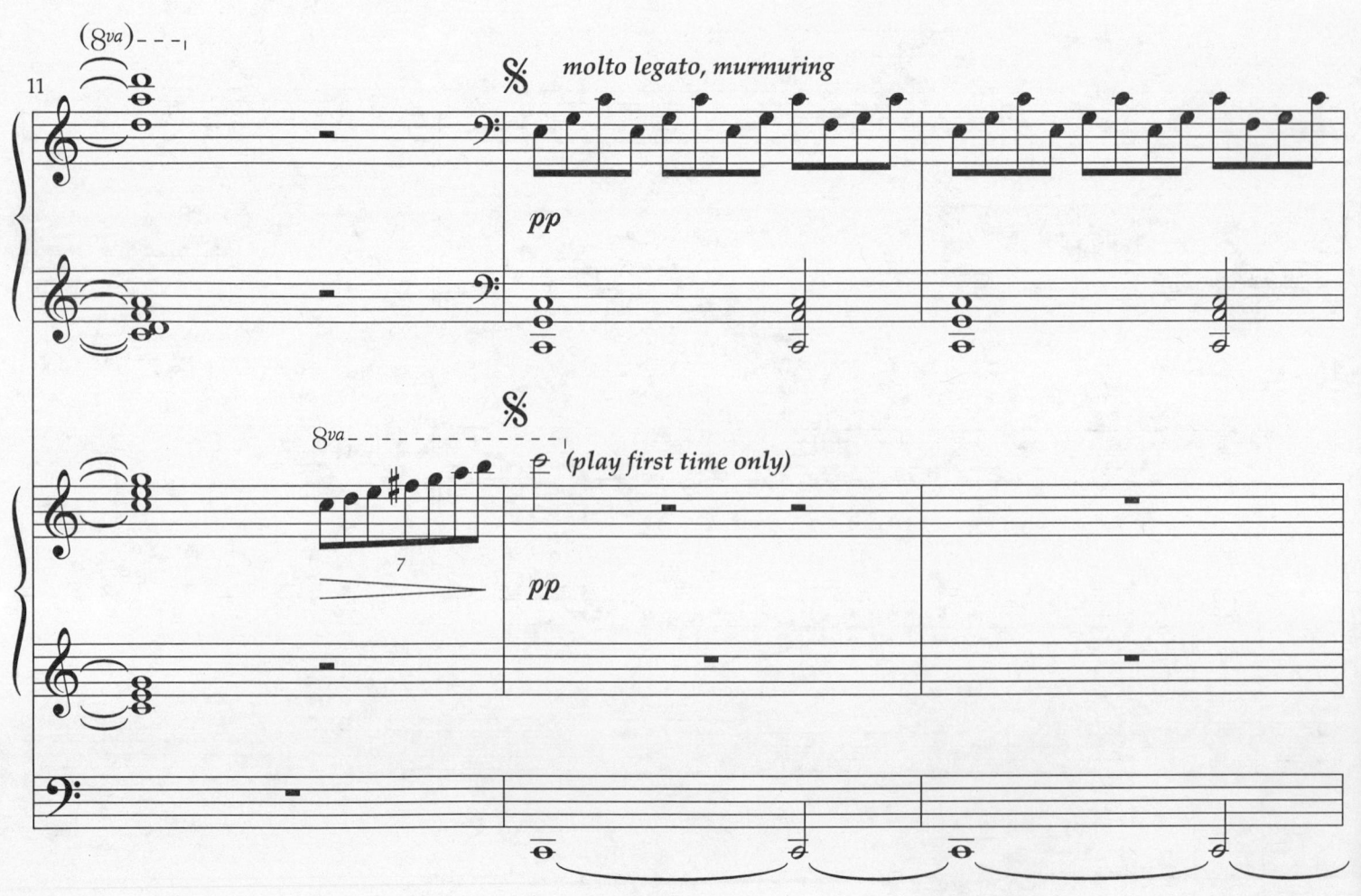

The Lord's My Shepherd — 2

The Lord's My Shepherd — 3

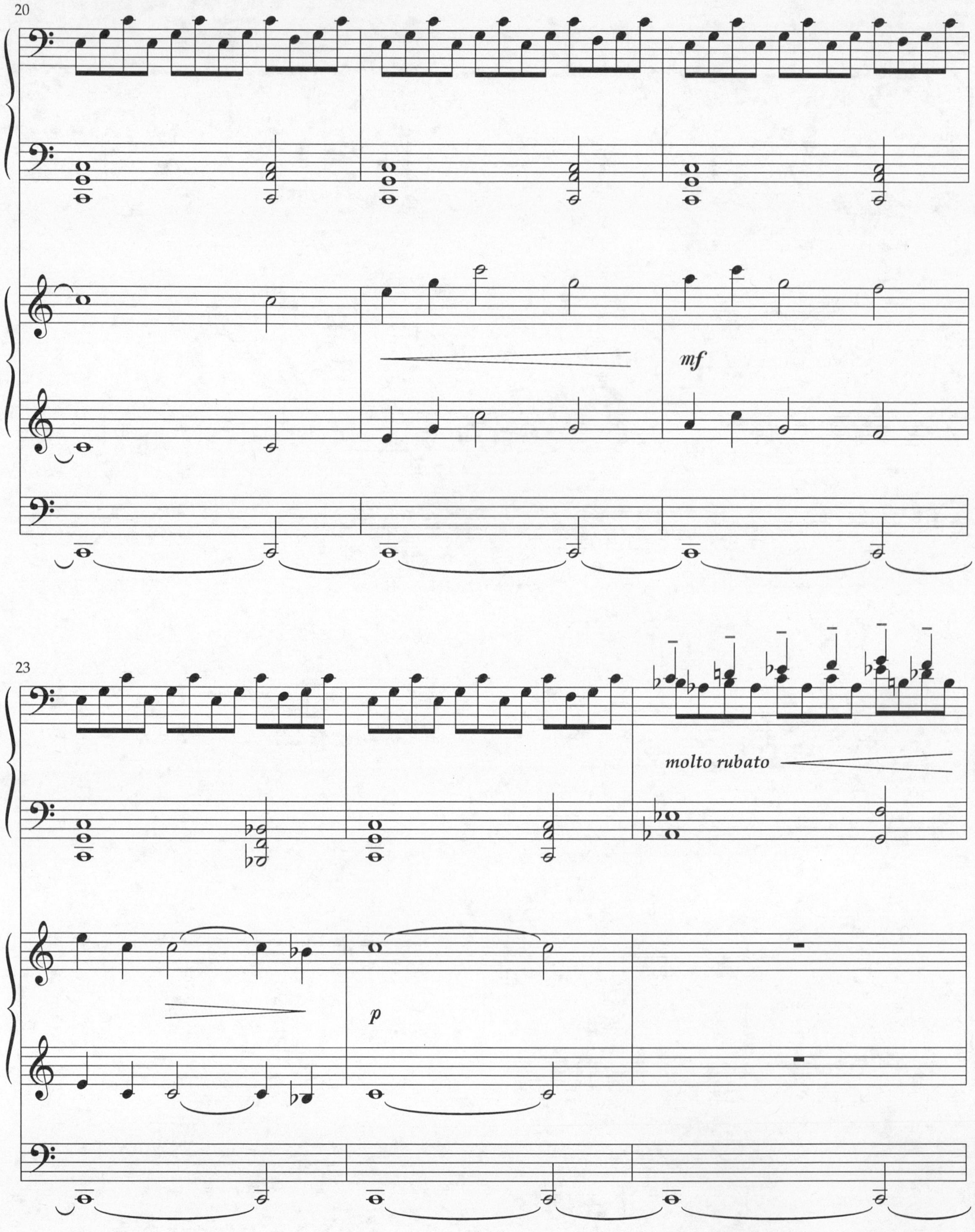
20
mf
23
molto rubato
p

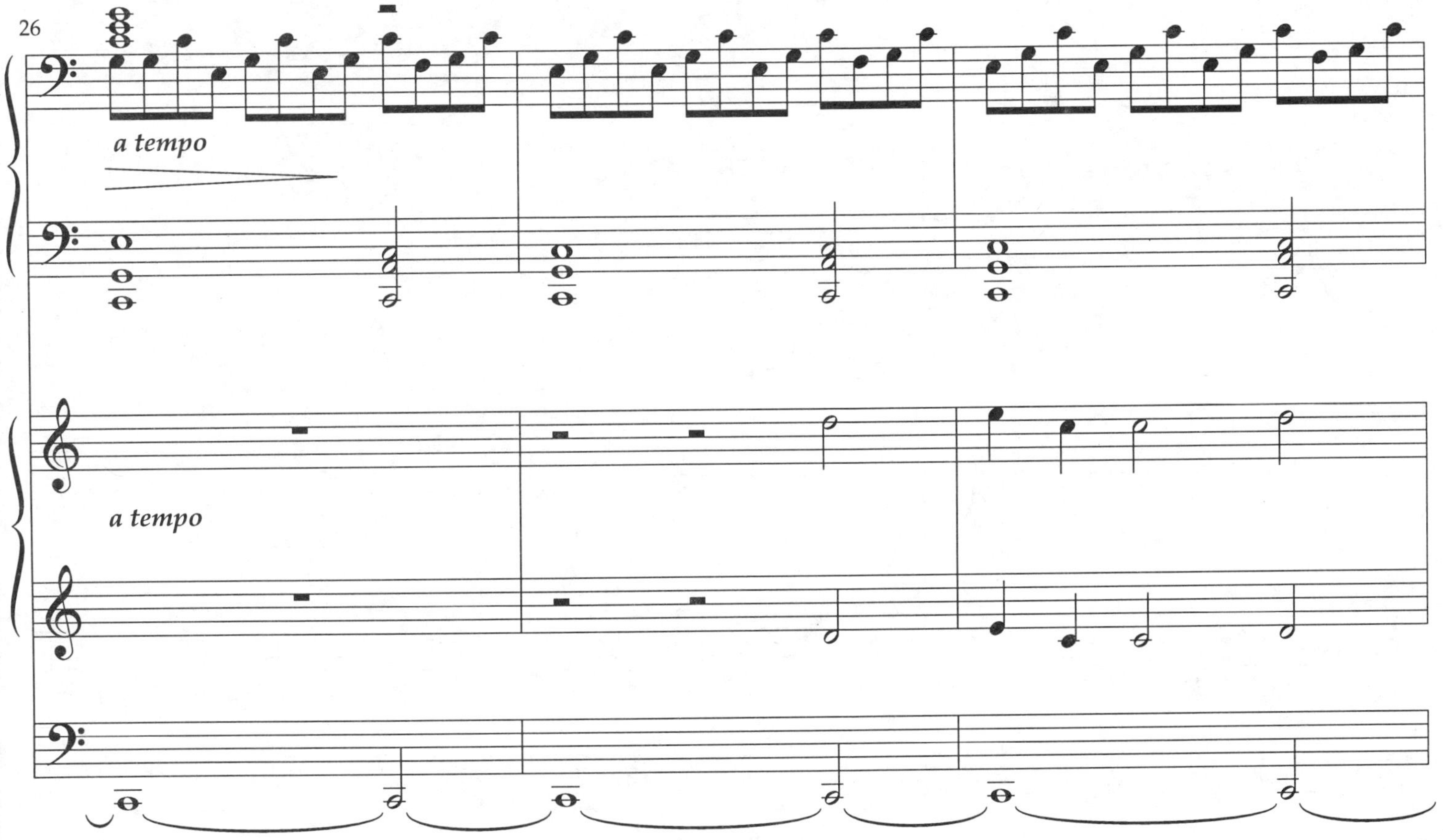
26
a tempo
a tempo

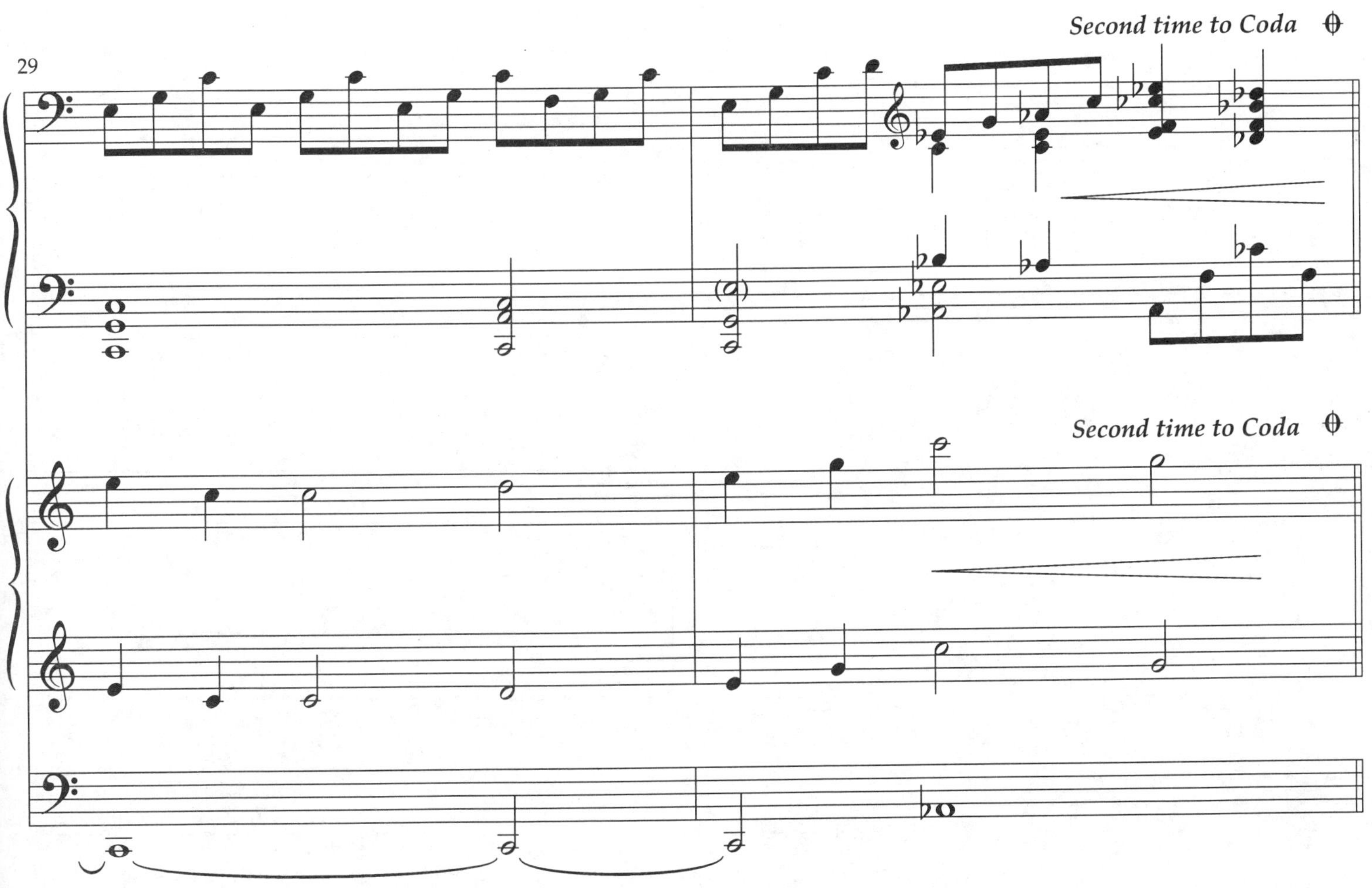
29
Second time to Coda
Second time to Coda

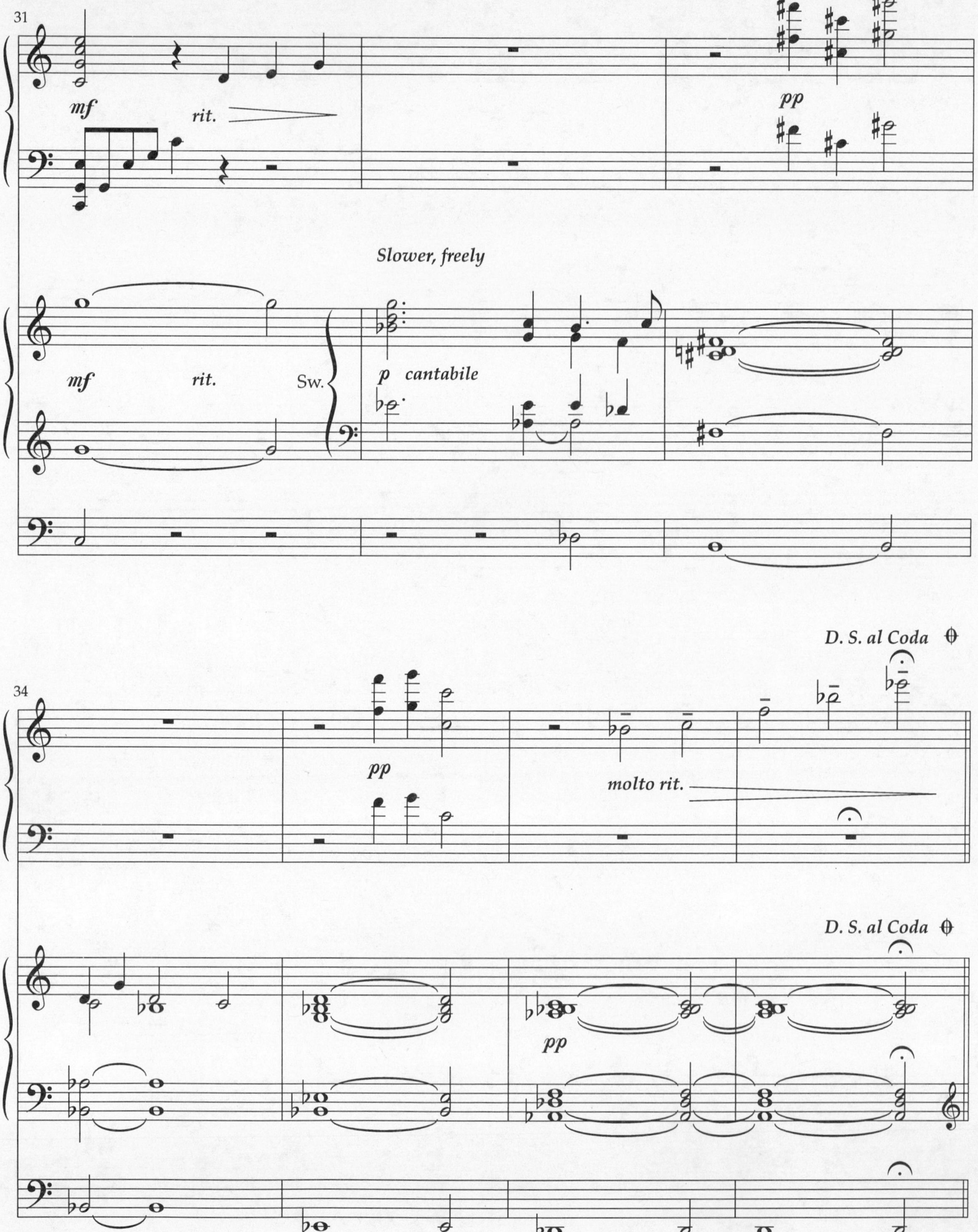
31
mf
rit.
pp
Slower, freely
mf
rit.
Sw.
p cantabile
34
D. S. al Coda
pp
molto rit.
D. S. al Coda
pp

38
CODA
Adagio
mf
molto rit.
molto rit.
mf
a tempo
dim.
CODA
mf molto rit.
molto rit.
a tempo
41
poco rit.
p
a tempo
poco rit.
Sw.
pp
Gt.
mf
a tempo
dim.
Sw.

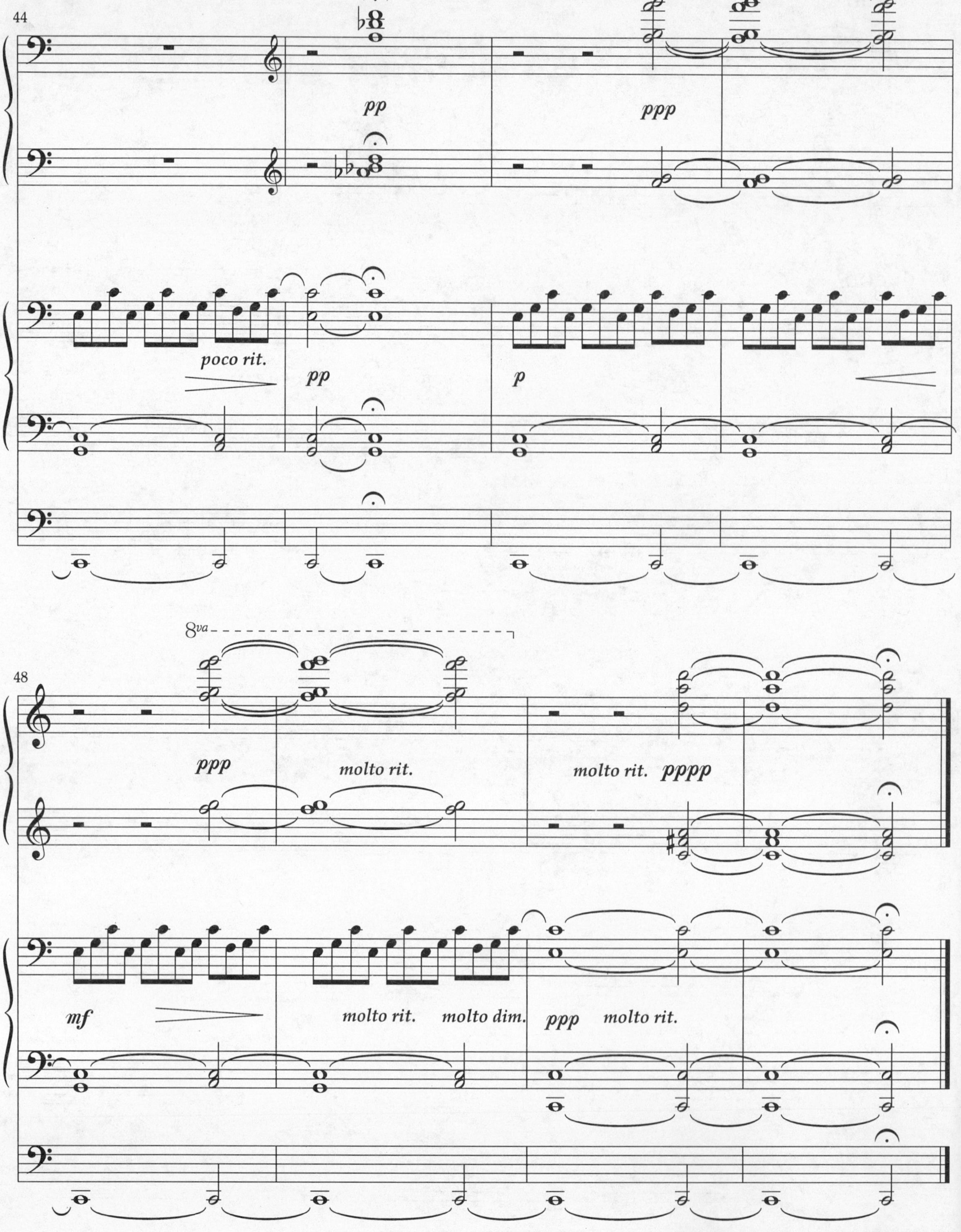
44
pp
ppp
poco rit.
pp
p
8va
48
ppp
molto rit.
molto rit.
pppp
mf
molto rit.
molto dim.
ppp
molto rit.

For Nielson and Young

Take Thou My Hand and Lead Me

Sw. Flutes 8' and 4'
Gt. Principals 8' and 4'
Ped. 16' and 8'

FRIEDRICH SILCHER
Duo-Piano Setting by
Kurt Kaiser

Expressively (♩. = 64)

© Copyright 1999 Kurt Kaiser Music. Adm. by The Copyright Co., Nashville, Tennessee.
All rights reserved. International copyright secured. Used by permission.

Take Thou My Hand and Lead Me — 2

slight accel. and cresc.

slight accel. and cresc.

Take Thou My Hand and Lead Me — 3

Take Thou My Hand and Lead Me — 4

Take Thou My Hand and Lead Me — 5

Take Thou My Hand and Lead Me — 6

Take Thou My Hand and Lead Me — 7

Take Thou My Hand and Lead Me — 8

Take Thou My Hand and Lead Me — 9

Redeemed
Ada

Sw. Flutes and Strings 8' and 4'
Gt. Principals 8', 4' and 2'
Ped. 16' and 8'

A. L. BUTLER
Piano-Organ Duet Setting by
Stephen Nielson and Ovid Young

© Copyright 1999 Van Ness Press, Inc. (ASCAP) in *Glorious Is Thy Name*.
Distributed by Church Street Music (a div. of GMG), Nashville, TN 37234.

Redeemed — 2

Redeemed — 3

Redeemed — 4

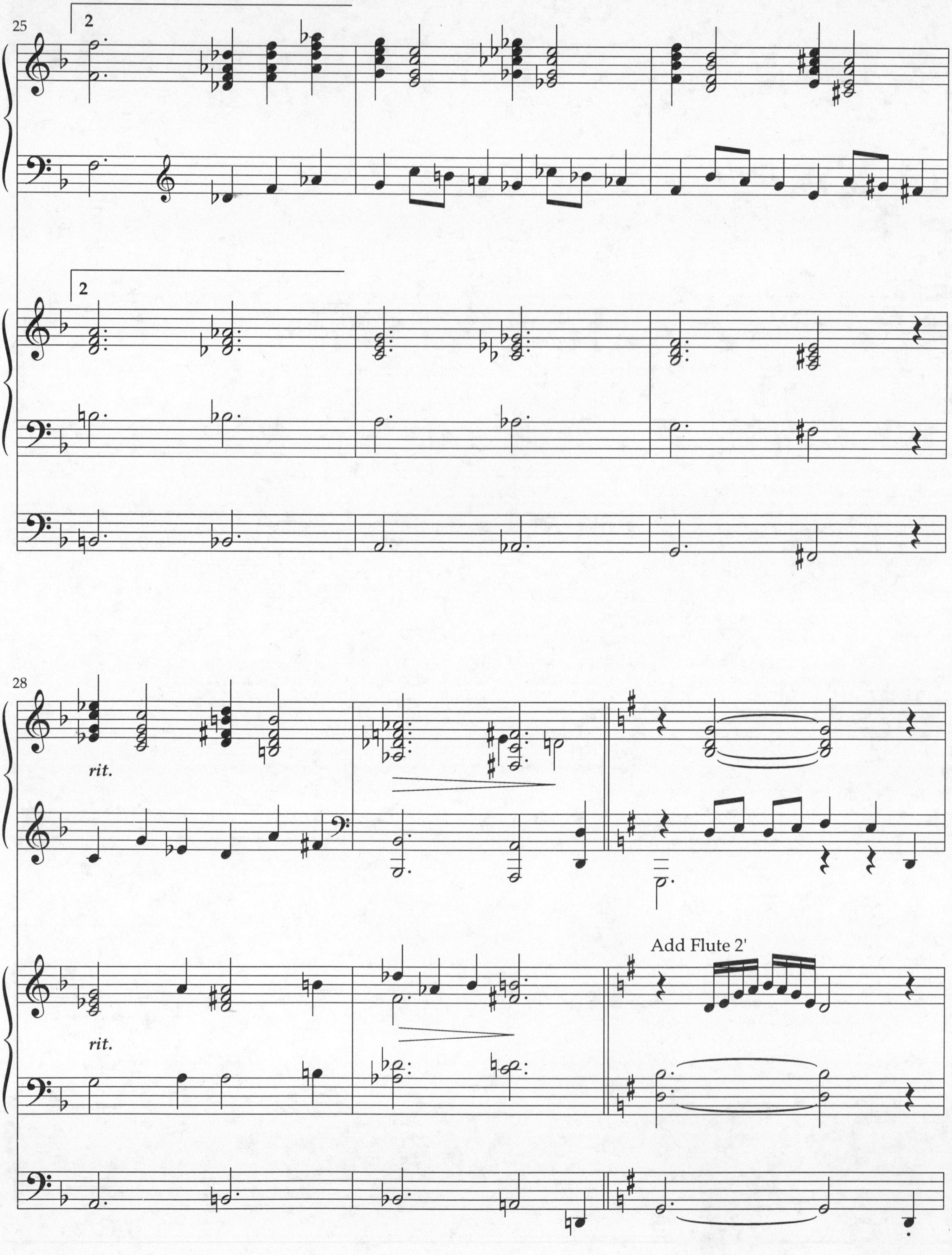
25
2
2
28
rit.
rit.
Add Flute 2'

Redeemed — 6

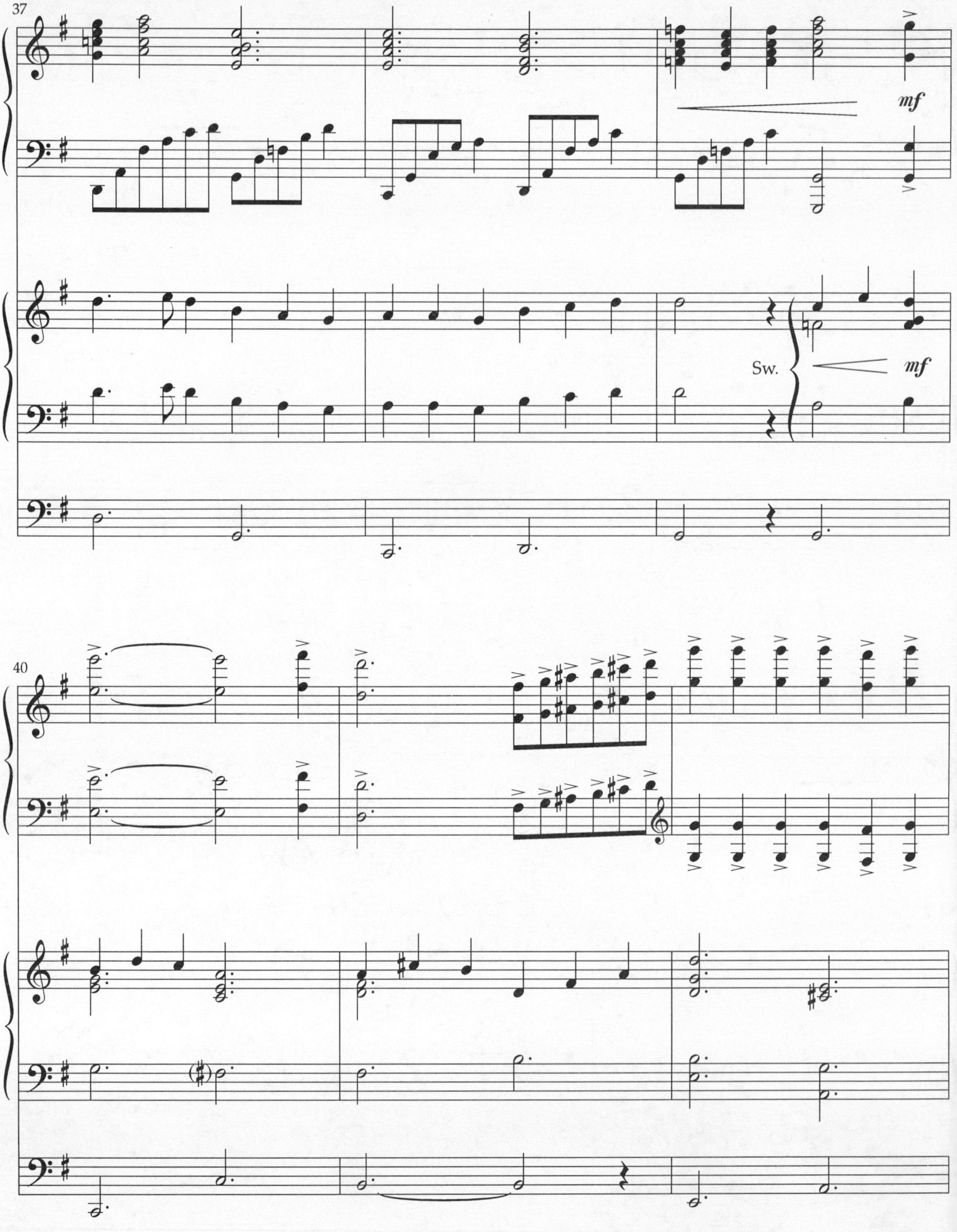
37
mf
Sw.
mf
40

Redeemed — 8

Redeemed — 9

Redeemed — 10

Come, Thou Fount of Every Blessing
Warrenton

Sw. Reed 8'
Gt. Principals 8' and 4'
Ped. 16' and 8'

The Sacred Harp, 1844
Piano-Organ Duet Setting by
Stephen Nielson and Ovid Young

© Copyright 1999 Van Ness Press, Inc. (ASCAP) in *Glorious Is Thy Name*.
Distributed by Church Street Music (a div. of GMG), Nashville, TN 37234.

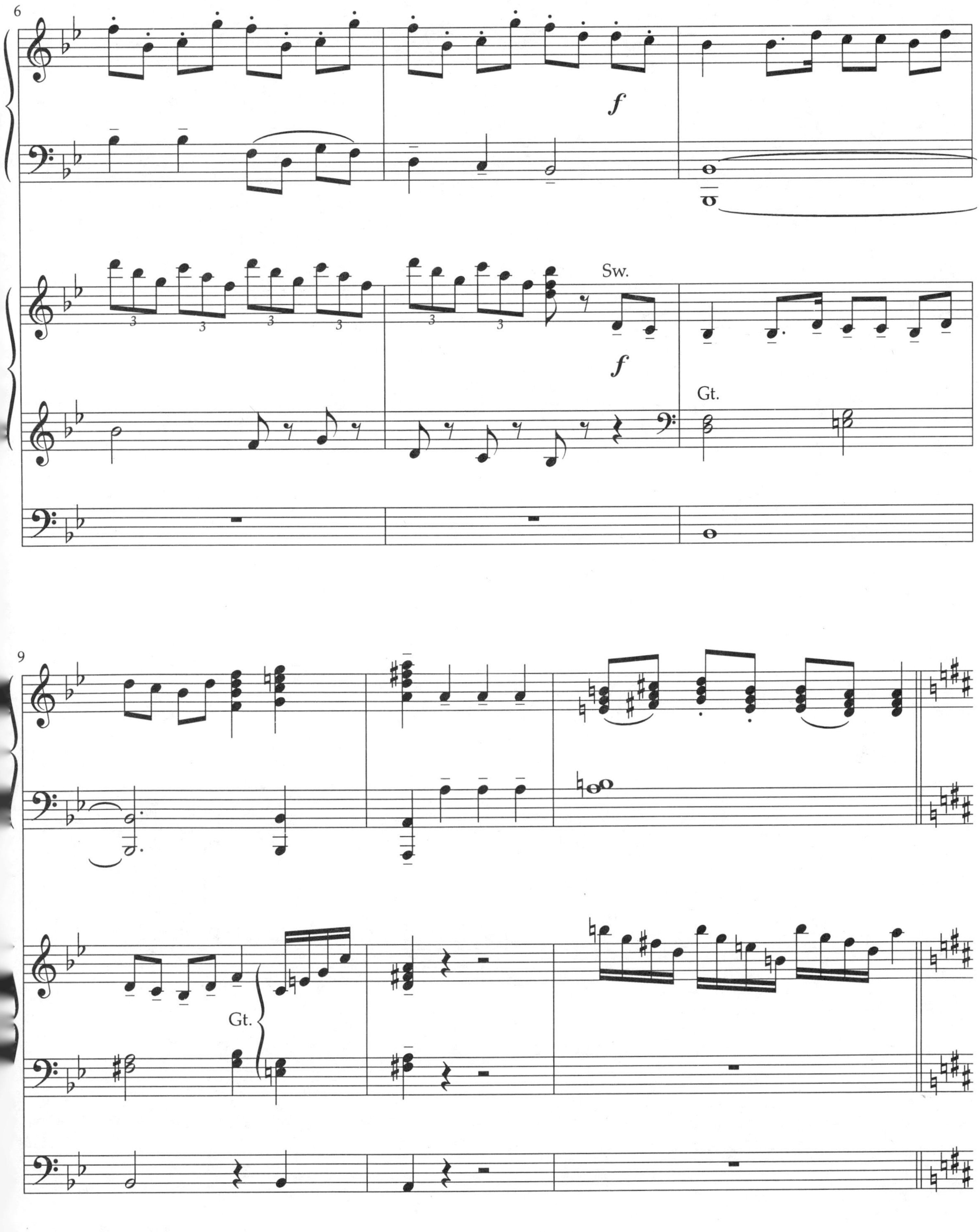
6
f
Sw.
f
Gt.
9
Gt.

Come, Thou Fount of Every Blessing — 3

Come, Thou Fount of Every Blessing — 4

Come, Thou Fount of Every Blessing — 5

Come, Thou Fount of Every Blessing — 6

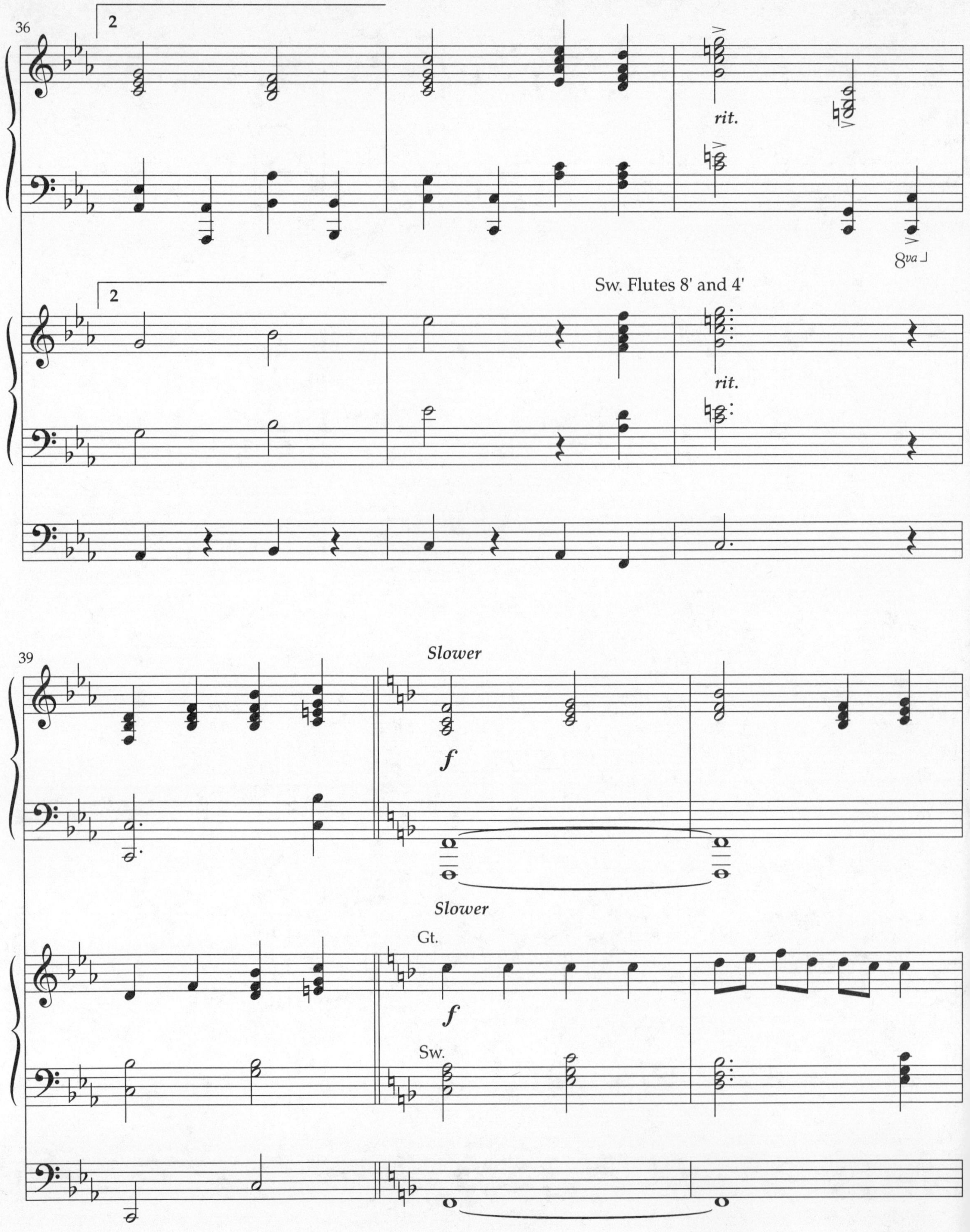
36
2
rit.
8va
2
Sw. Flutes 8' and 4'
rit.
39
Slower
f
Slower
Gt.
f
Sw.

Come, Thou Fount of Every Blessing — 8

Come, Thou Fount of Every Blessing — 9

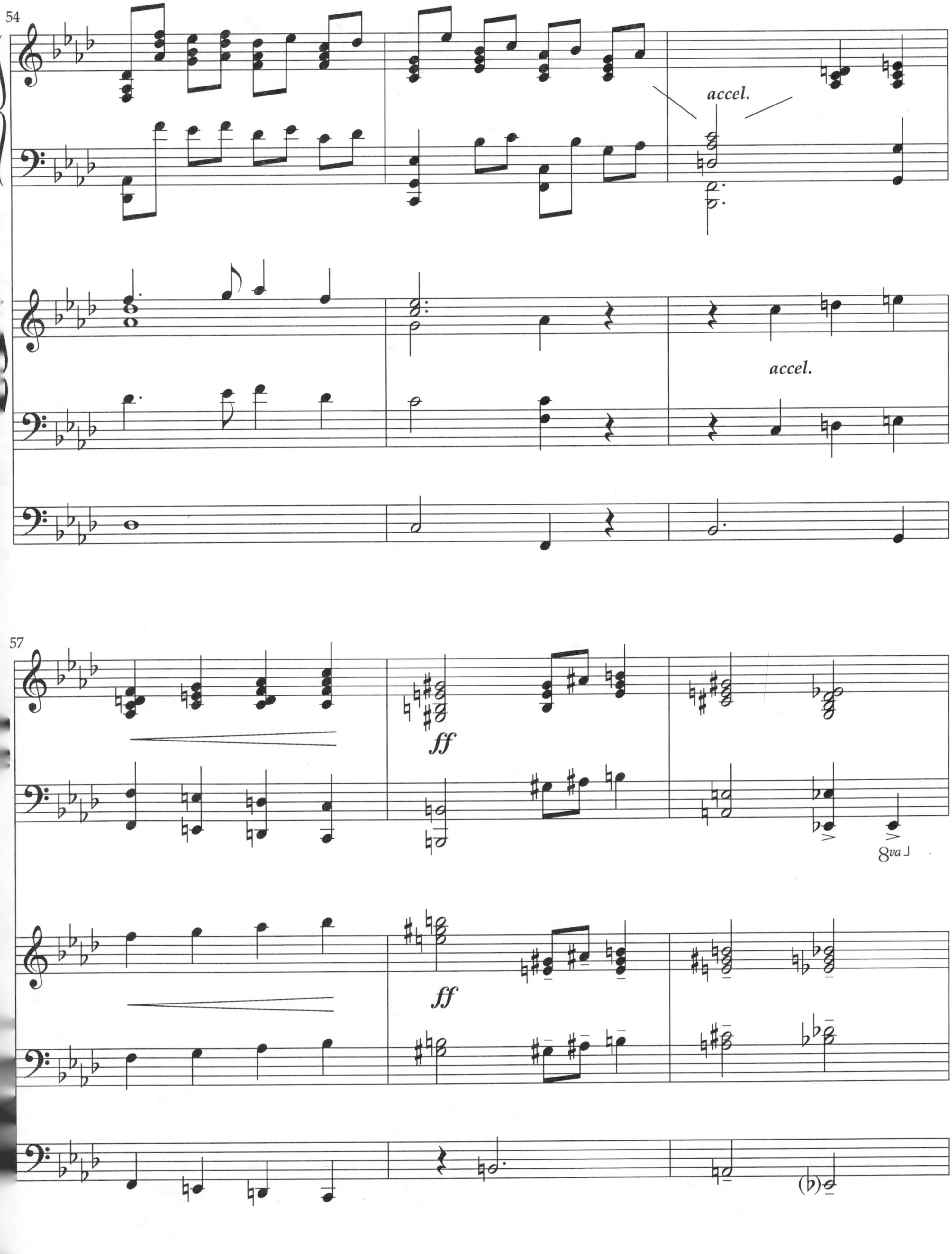
54
accel.
accel.
57
ff
ff
8va

Come, Thou Fount of Every Blessing — 11

All Glory, Laud, and Honor — 8

70
p
subito
ff
molto marcato
subito
molto marcato
p
ff
72
8va
ff
molto rit.
ff
molto rit.
8va
8va
75
a tempo
8va
sfz
no rit.
fff
sfz
8va
8va
a tempo
no rit.
fff
sfz
8va

Praise God, from Whom All Blessings Flow
Old 100th

Genevan Psalter, 1551 Edition
Duo-Piano Setting by
Stephen Nielson and Ovid Young

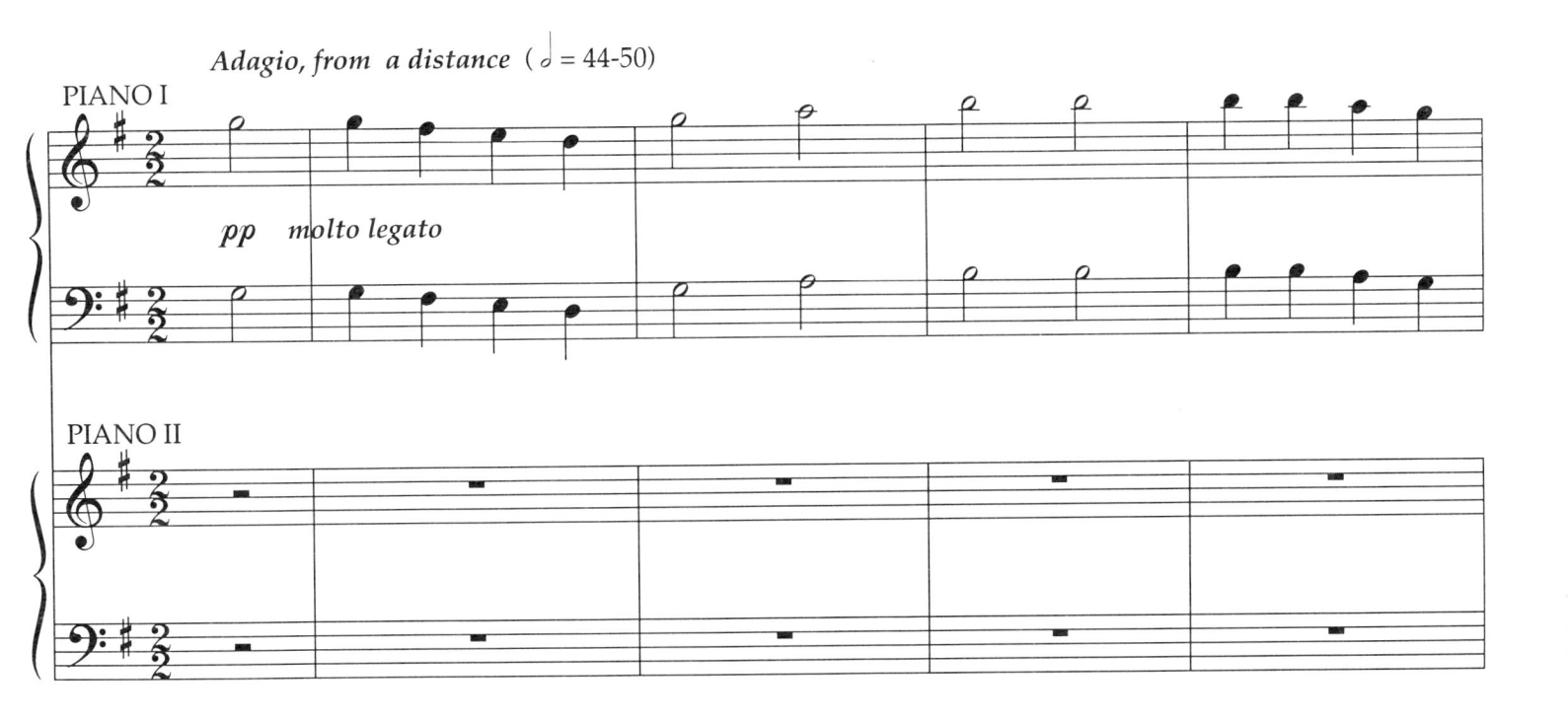

Adagio, from a distance (♩ = 44-50)

pp molto legato

© Copyright 1999 Van Ness Press, Inc. (ASCAP) in *Glorious Is Thy Name*.
Distributed by Church Street Music (a div. of GMG), Nashville, TN 37234.

10
ff con forza
14
molto rit.
8va
molto rit.
8va
8va
19
Allegro, with energy (♩ = 116-132)
f
ff

Praise God, from Whom All Blessings Flow — 3

Praise God, from Whom All Blessings Flow — 4

Praise God, from Whom All Blessings Flow — 5

8va
45
ff molto rit.
ff molto rit.
8va
47
(♩ = 120-138)
f Più mosso to end, with no rit.
f Più mosso to end, with no rit.
49
fff
15ma
5
fff
15ma
sfz
5

The Lord's My Shepherd
Brother James' Air

J. L. MacBETH BAIN
Duo-Piano Setting by
Stephen Nielson and Ovid Young

*Based on Arabesque #1 by Claude Debussy.

© Copyright 1999 Van Ness Press, Inc. (ASCAP) in *Glorious Is Thy Name*.
Distributed by Church Street Music (a div. of GMG), Nashville, TN 37234.

7
8va
mp
Ped.
Ped.
(8va)
11
molto legato, murmuring
pp
8va
7
mp
(play first time only)
pp
14
8va
p

The Lord's My Shepherd — 3

26
a tempo
29
Second time to Coda
8va
Second time to Coda
31
mf
rit.
pp
Slower, freely
mf
rit.
p cantabile

The Lord's My Shepherd — 5

43
a tempo
pp
mf
a tempo
dim.
poco rit.
pp
46
8va
ppp
ppp
p
cresc.
mf
49
(8va)
molto rit.
molto rit.
pppp
molto rit.
molto dim.
ppp
molto rit.
8va

For Nielson and Young

Take Thou My Hand and Lead Me

FRIEDRICH SILCHER
Duo-Piano Setting by
Kurt Kaiser

© Copyright 1999 Kurt Kaiser Music. Adm. by The Copyright Co., Nashville, Tennessee.
All rights reserved. International copyright secured. Used by permission.

Take Thou My Hand and Lead Me — 2

Tempo as before

Tempo as before

Take Thou My Hand and Lead Me — 3

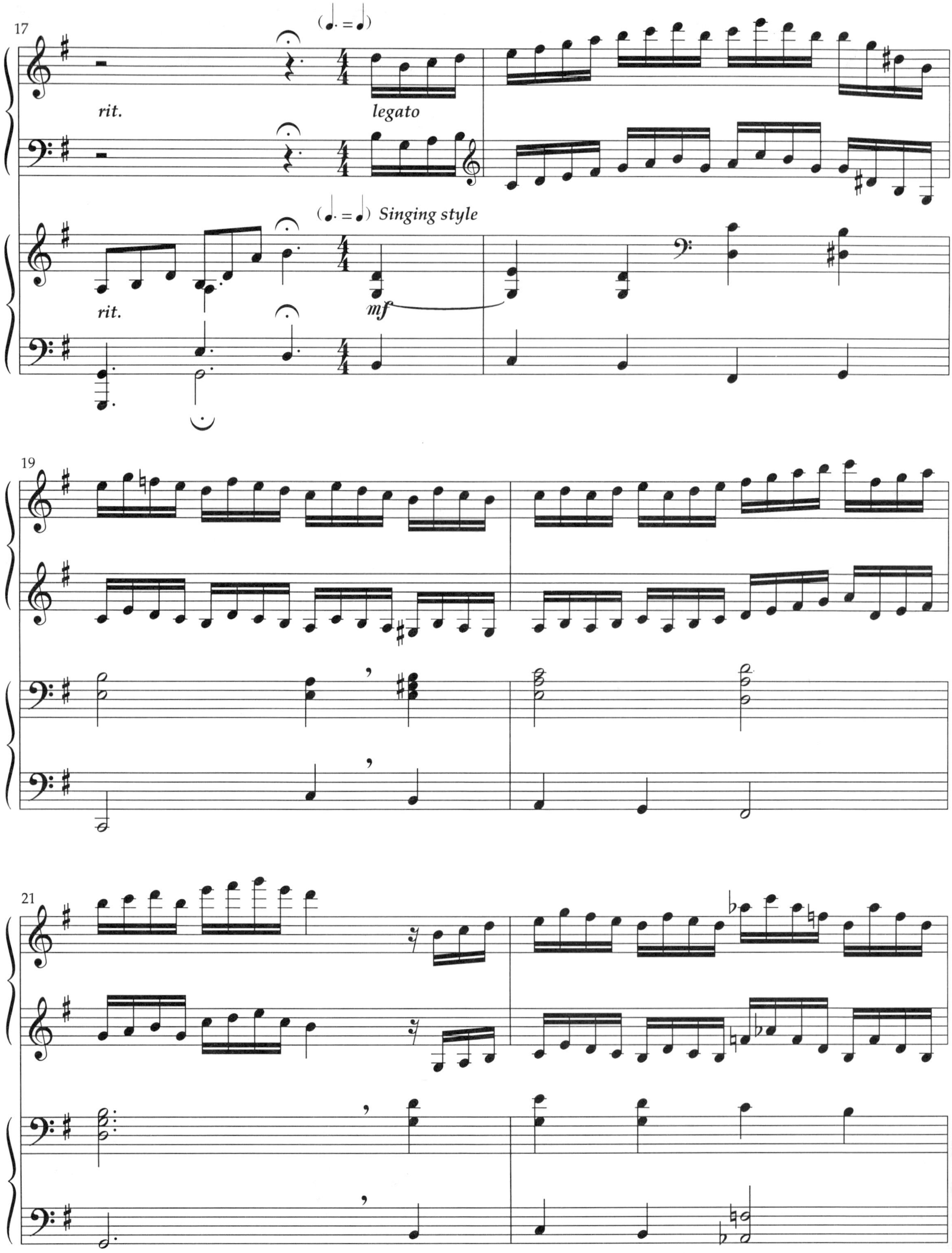

17
(♩. = ♩)
rit.
legato
(♩. = ♩) Singing style
rit.
mf
19
21

Take Thou My Hand and Lead Me — 5

Take Thou My Hand and Lead Me — 6

Take Thou My Hand and Lead Me — 7

Redeemed
Ada

A. L. BUTLER
Duo-Piano Setting by
Stephen Nielson and Ovid Young

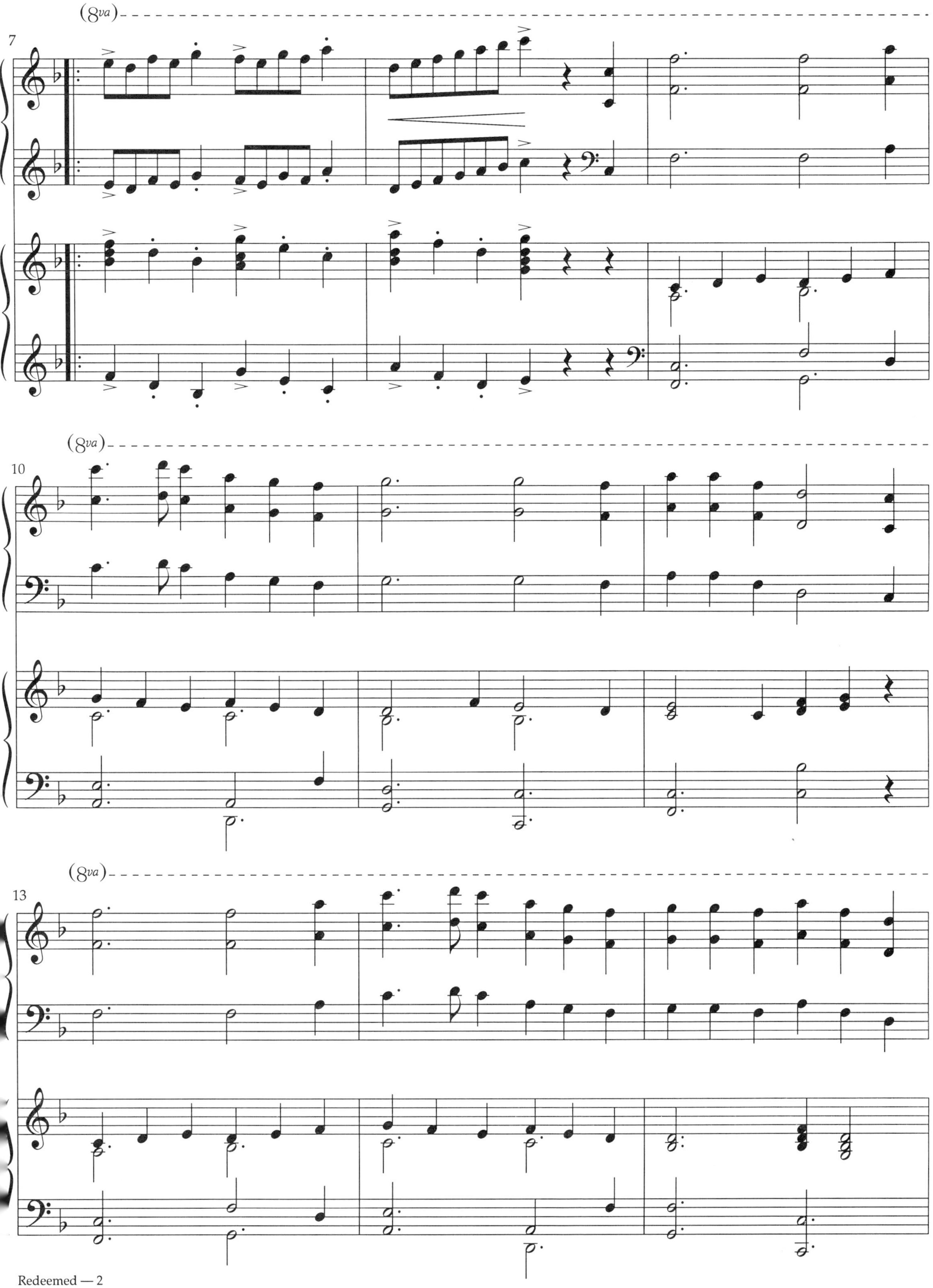
(8va)
7
(8va)
10
(8va)
13

Redeemed — 3

Redeemed — 4

Redeemed — 5

63

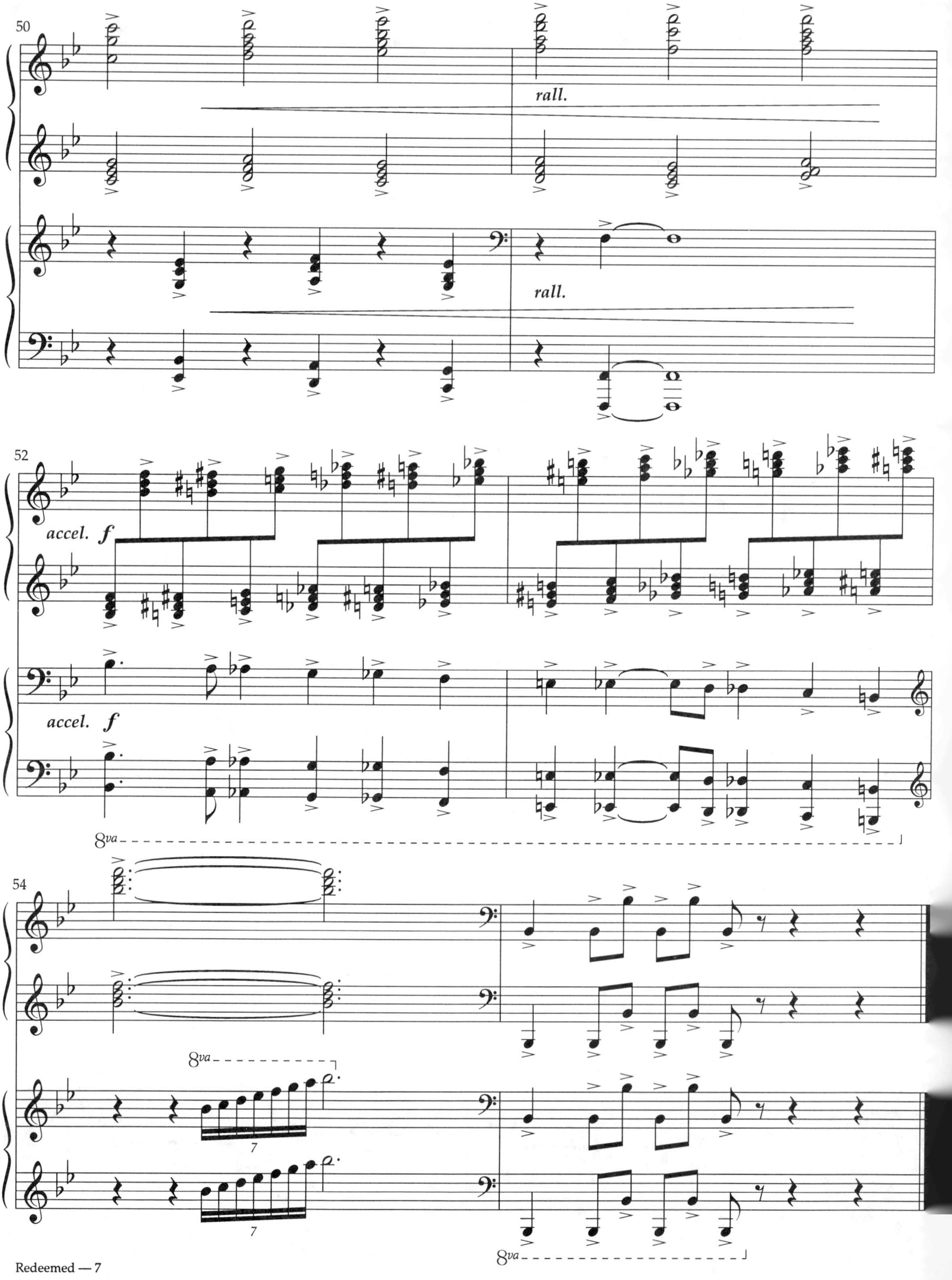
50
rall.
rall.
52
accel.
f
accel.
f
8va
54
8va
7
7
8va

Come, Thou Fount of Every Blessing

Warrenton

The Sacred Harp, 1844
Duo-Piano Setting by
Stephen Nielson and Ovid Young

© Copyright 1999 Van Ness Press, Inc. (ASCAP) in *Glorious Is Thy Name.*
Distributed by Church Street Music (a div. of GMG), Nashville, TN 37234.

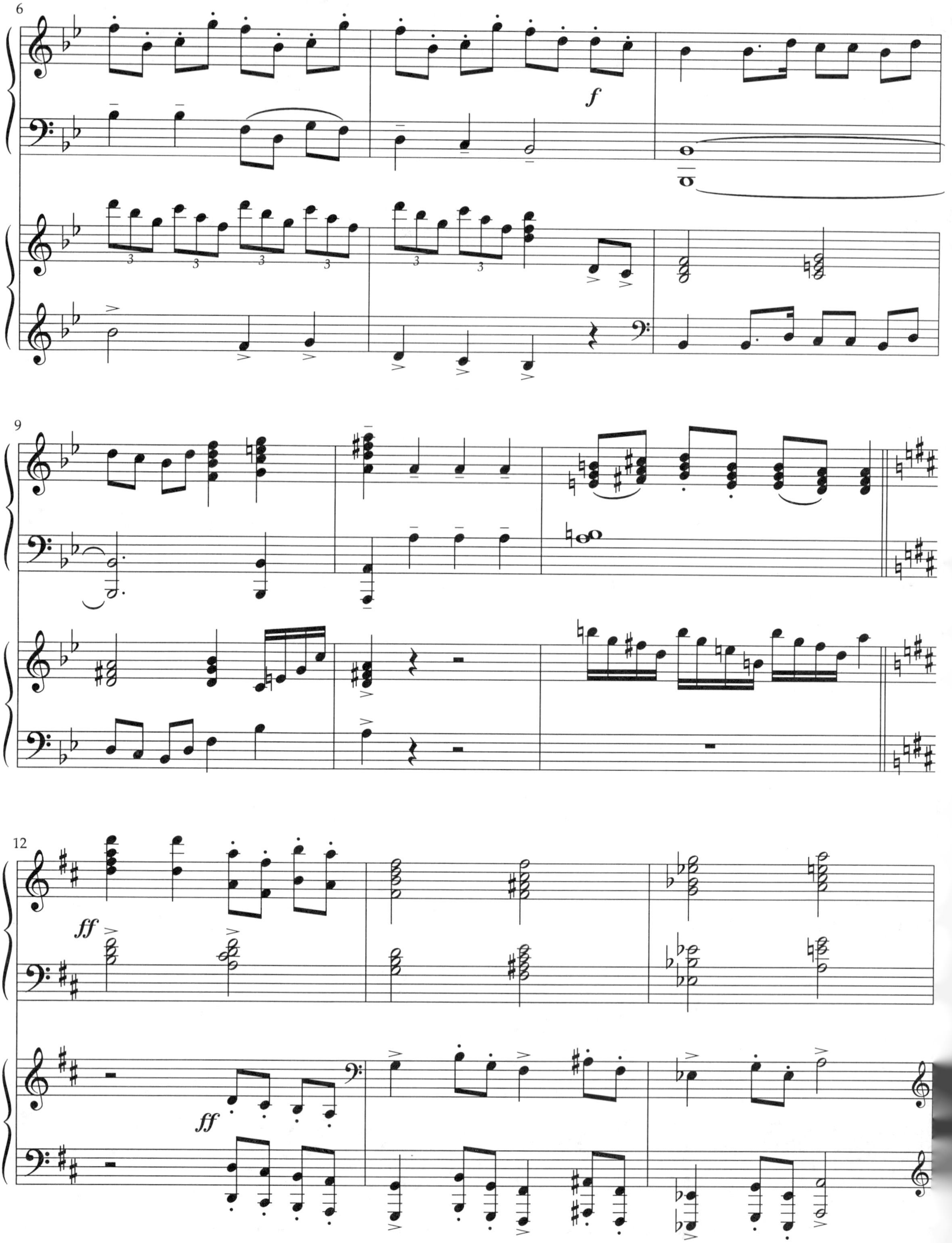
6
f
9
12
ff
ff

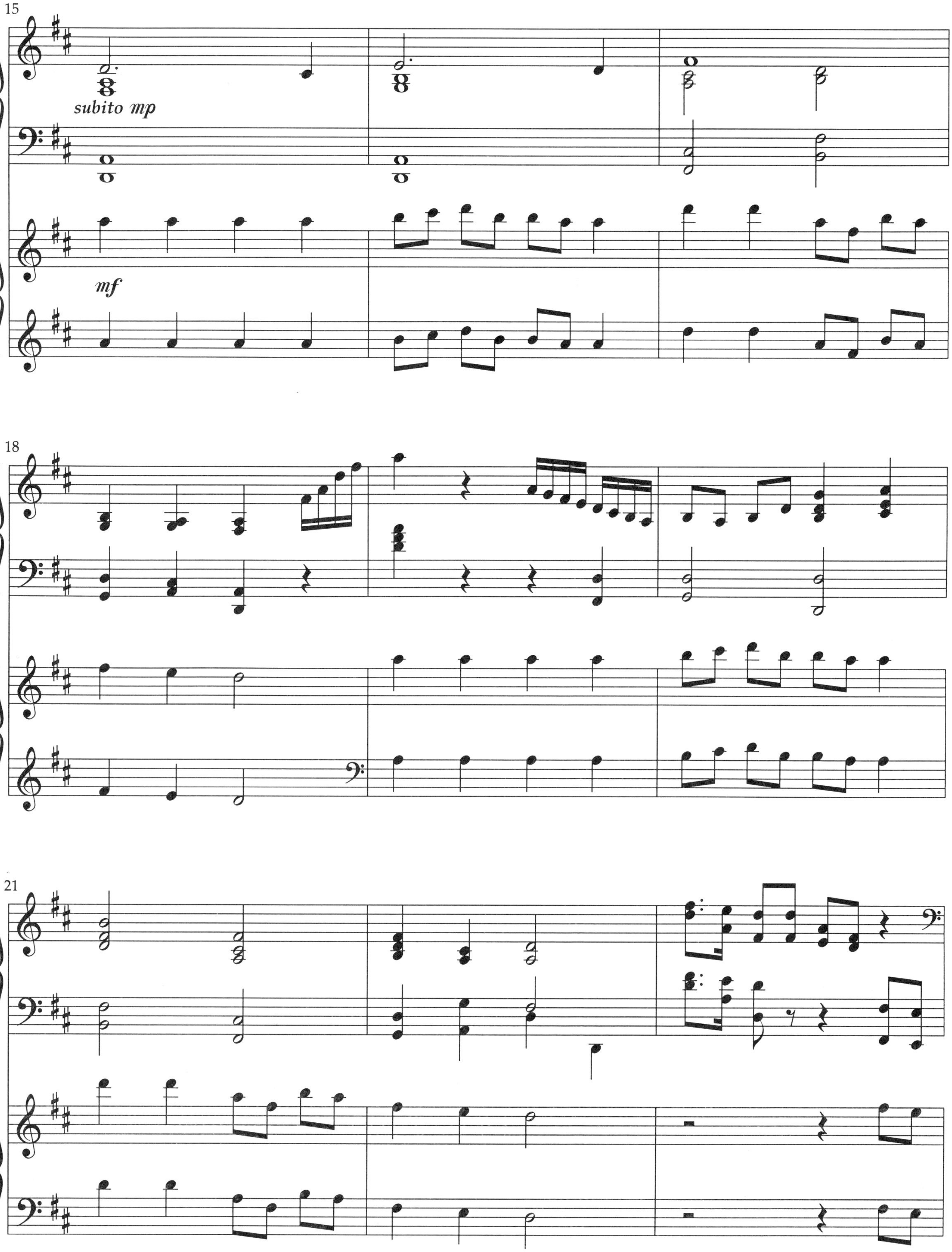
15
subito mp
mf
18
21

Come, Thou Fount of Every Blessing — 4

Come, Thou Fount of Every Blessing — 5

cresc. poco a poco

Come, Thou Fount of Every Blessing — 6

Come, Thou Fount of Every Blessing — 7

Come, Thou Fount of Every Blessing — 8